Concerto of Crows and Cowards

Dynamis Security

Liliana Hart

Copyright © 2024 by Liliana Hart

All rights reserved.

Published by 7th Press
Dallas, TX 75115

All rights reserved. This book or any portion thereof may not be reproduced or used in any manner whatsoever without the express written permission of the author except for the use of brief quotations in a book review.

This is a work of fiction. Names, characters, businesses, places, events and incidents are either the products of the author's imagination or used in a fictitious manner. Any resemblance to actual persons, living or dead, or actual events is purely coincidental.

Also by Liliana Hart

JJ Graves Mystery Series

Dirty Little Secrets

A Dirty Shame

Dirty Rotten Scoundrel

Down and Dirty

Dirty Deeds

Dirty Laundry

Dirty Money

A Dirty Job

Dirty Devil

Playing Dirty

Dirty Martini

Dirty Dozen

Dirty Minds

Dirty Weekend

Dirty Looks

Addison Holmes Mystery Series

Whiskey Rebellion

Whiskey Sour

Whiskey For Breakfast

Whiskey, You're The Devil

Whiskey on the Rocks

Whiskey Tango Foxtrot

Whiskey and Gunpowder

Whiskey Lullaby

The Scarlet Chronicles

Bouncing Betty

Hand Grenade Helen

Front Line Francis

The Harley and Davidson Mystery Series

The Farmer's Slaughter

A Tisket a Casket

I Saw Mommy Killing Santa Claus

Get Your Murder Running

Deceased and Desist

Malice in Wonderland

Tequila Mockingbird

Gone With the Sin

Grime and Punishment

Blazing Rattles

A Salt and Battery

Curl Up and Dye

First Comes Death Then Comes Marriage

Box Set 1

Box Set 2

Box Set 3

The Gravediggers

The Darkest Corner

Gone to Dust

Say No More

Laurel Valley

Tribulation Pass

Redemption Road

Midnight Clear

Prologue

Five Years Ago…

"I'm pregnant."

Jade Jax stared at herself in the mirror—wide green eyes tinged with a hint of shock and panic. She knew if she didn't practice saying the words aloud, she'd never get them out when it was time to do it for real. So much for birth control.

Nausea rolled through her and she gritted her teeth and breathed out slowly, trying to delay the inevitable. Her face was pale and clammy, and she'd become good friends with the end stall in the ladies' room in the Department of Justice building over the past three weeks.

"Dammit." She raced into the stall and

emptied what was left in her stomach. It was only vaguely annoying she'd been in there often enough to notice one of the floor tiles was cracked in the shape of the Virgin Mary. Mostly it just reminded her she needed to pray. Then maybe she could put something in her stomach without it reappearing again.

She stumbled back to the sink and splashed cold water onto her face, and then she wetted a few paper towels and let the cold trickle down the middle of her breasts. She had to pull herself together. There was less than two hours until go time. The next mission was an important one, and Max would detain her and make her stay stateside if he thought she was sick—even if it was her own husband who was the mission.

Donovan Jax had been in deep cover inside Alexander Ramos's organization for the last eighteen months. It was a dangerous job—a job she'd begged him not to take. They'd fought over it for weeks, but in the end she'd lost the battle. Donovan felt he was the right man for the job—the only person who could infiltrate the organization and pass on vital information to the DEA. And the hard part was accepting he was right. He was a good man, a good agent, and justice would always be more important than his safety. Falling in love with a hero was hell.

Their time together over the last year and a half had been sparse—stolen weekends in remote locations where they hadn't wasted time talking but instead had fallen straight into bed. When the time was added up, they'd actually been apart longer than they'd been married. It had been four weeks since she'd seen him last—four weeks since they'd made love. And made a baby.

Her hand went to her stomach protectively. Maybe this baby was a sign. She and the rest of the team were flying down to extract Donovan from Mexico. The assignment had gotten too dangerous, and Ramos was beginning to suspect some of his top men of betraying him. More than one body of his known lieutenants had been found—at least what had been left of them.

Don't think about it. He's coming home.

The DEA had enough information to begin the process of ending Ramos's reign forever. Donovan would come home, and they could be a family without threats or danger hanging over their heads at every turn. In fact, maybe it was time to turn in her badge and her weapon. The past ten years felt more like fifty, and the weight of the world was getting awfully heavy—not to mention the rifle she had to use much too frequently.

The more she thought about it, the more she knew it was the right decision. Max would throw a fit, but he could find another agent to replace her. The child growing inside of her couldn't grow up without a mother if anything happened to her.

Jade patted her face dry with a towel and slapped her cheeks for a little color. She had a mission to prepare for, and it was the most important mission of her life. Donovan was coming home.

"I'm pregnant," she said one last time to the mirror. This time she couldn't help but smile.

———

The DEA offices were on the fifth floor of the Department of Justice building, and she headed down the long gray corridor to her small office.

They were supposed to meet at 14:30 for a briefing before the plane took off. She had just enough time to change clothes and check her weapons one final time.

Her office was a small square dominated by a metal desk. The floors were gray industrial-grade carpet and the walls were stark white. A bookshelf stood in the corner, and the shelves bowed under the weight of books—anything from nonfiction to thrillers to the romances she kept on the bottom shelf so the guys wouldn't give her a hard time. She spent more time at work than home anyway, so it made sense to have the things she enjoyed close by. A green plant flourished on the corner of her desk, and pictures sat on every free surface. It was a cramped and overflowing space, but she wouldn't trade it for anything. It was hers. And having things that belonged solely to her was something she'd learned to treasure.

Jade pulled her pack from the bottom drawer of her desk and changed into black cargo pants and a long-sleeved black T-shirt. She pulled the pins from her hair and let it fall around her shoulders, brushing it out quickly before pulling it back in a ponytail. Maybe it was time to cut it short. She wouldn't want to deal with the hassle of long hair when the baby was born.

Jade checked the magazine in her Sig and pocketed another two, but her pride and joy was in the long black case under her desk. She pulled it out and set it on top of her desk, flicking open the locks with her thumbs and pushing back the lid. The M40A3 rifle gleamed back at her—the black so smooth and polished she could see her reflection in it.

The knock on her door had her yelling out, "Enter," and she closed the lid on the case with a snap.

She knew something was wrong the moment Max stepped inside and closed the door behind him. Max was a good boss and a great agent, and she knew his responsibility weighed heavily on him. He truly cared about his agents, and he'd flip his middle finger to the bureaucrats and politicians if it meant those under his command were going to get screwed. There weren't many she'd trust to watch her back if things went to hell, but he was one of them.

But the Max she'd worked with the last few years was almost unrecognizable in the man who stood before her. His face was drawn and his eyes shadowed with grief. His hair was disheveled as if he'd been running his fingers through it, and his normally impeccable clothes were wrinkled—his tie shoved in his pocket and the collar of his shirt unbuttoned.

"What's wrong?" Her voice was foreign to her ears. Her palms slicked with sweat and her lungs felt as if they were bursting in her chest. Somewhere deep inside she knew—knew that whatever Max had to say would break her.

She wiped her palms on her pants and shook her head, coming around the desk to face him head-on.

"Jade," he said. And she knew. She knew Donovan was dead, as if someone had flicked a switch off inside of her.

"No, you're wrong." Her soul was splintering into pieces and he expected her to just believe him, without proof. "You'll see. We can leave early and go get him. We'll do the extraction and you'll see he's okay. We'll bring him home." Her voice rose higher and higher as panic took over. She was trained to never panic —to breathe deep and keep her focus. But she couldn't do it this time. She just couldn't.

"I'm sorry, Jade." Max reached out for her, but she moved back, knocking the picture frame from her desk to the floor. Glass crunched beneath her feet, and she bent down to salvage what was left of her wedding photo.

Glass sliced at her finger and blood welled instantly, but she pulled the picture from the shards and held it against her breast.

"No," she said again. "No, no, no. It's just a misunderstanding. I want to talk to our contacts in Mexico. I want someone to go in and bring him out now. If he's in danger, then we don't need to waste a minute."

Max knelt down beside her and held her trembling hands. The blood from the cut on her finger welled faster, soaking into the white cuff of his shirt.

"He's gone, Jade." His voice cracked, and he had to swallow a couple of times before he could go on. "I've spent the last three hours trying to cut through red tape and lies to get the answers I needed. Let me get this out," he said. "You know I have to say the words."

She shook her head, but it didn't stop him from speaking. "I'm sorry for your loss. Donovan Jax was killed in the line of duty."

"I said no!" she screamed. Her fist connected with the side of his face before she could control it, as if someone else had taken over her body. She scrambled away, knocking over one of the folding chairs she had against the wall. Her hip hit the corner of her desk, but the pain didn't penetrate.

"Get out, get out!" Tears clouded her vision, but she grabbed the first thing she saw—the plant in the ceramic pot—and threw it at his head. Max dodged and got to his feet, but he didn't try to stop the storm brewing inside of her. The look of sympathy on his face only made the tears fall faster. God, she never cried. Not when she'd been shuffled from one foster home to the next and not when a bullet had pierced her flesh.

The door to her office opened and worried faces peeked in.

"Get out," Max said, and they closed the door with a snap.

Blood trickled from the corner of his mouth, but he was still and silent, letting her rage around him until there was nothing left inside of her but despair. Her breath heaved in and out of her lungs and she let her arms hang down at her side as a sudden weakness seemed to overtake her. Her head dropped down and a chill settled over her skin, making her shiver uncontrollably.

"I want to see him," she said, her voice breaking. "I need to see him."

"Oh, baby," Max said, coming toward her. She let him gather her close, so her head rested on his shoulder. He was grieving too. She could feel the fine tremors coursing through his body. Max and Donovan had been close—as close as most brothers. "You know I can't do that."

"Don't play games with me, Max. I don't care about the red tape or expense reports. I want his body brought back here. I need to see him."

His arms wrapped tight around her and he buried his head against her shoulder. She felt the heat of his tears against her neck, and she tightened her own hold around him, trying to comfort the both of them.

"I can't, Jade." He paused for a few seconds. "There's nothing left of him to bring home."

Something broke inside of her—an agony that started in her womb and ripped and clawed its way through her body. She would have doubled over if Max hadn't been holding her upright. Liquid rushed between her thighs and the coppery scent of blood filled the air.

She tried to scream, but the pain had taken control of her body, rendering her useless.

"Jade!" Max cried out, catching her as her knees gave out and she crumpled to the floor.

She'd lived through unspeakable tragedy in her life—the death of her parents when she was a child, the loss of friends she'd worked and served with, wounds, betrayal, and the loss of her husband—a man she'd loved with everything she'd had to give. But she'd never wanted to die before—not until she lost the only piece of Donovan she had left—the child she'd already imagined to have Donovan's wide grin and her green eyes.

Now there was nothing but blackness as the pain lessened and a cold numbness filled her body. In the back of her mind she thought she heard Max yelling something, calling her name, but she ignored it and embraced the cold. A smile touched her lips when she saw Donovan's face—one last time.

Six Months Later…

His body hurt. Everywhere.

It felt like his brain was caught in quicksand—his every thought disappearing into darkness just when he thought he finally had a good hold. He remembered being in Mexico with the team, on the search and rescue for an American hostage. And he remembered looking into the black eyes of Alexander Ramos just before Ramos pulled the trigger and hit Max in the leg as he dived to the side. The bullet had burned like fire, and he'd felt the crack of bone as the bullet lodged in his thigh. The last thing Max remembered was Ramos's arm around the hostage's throat and the gun in his hand pointed right at Max's head. He hadn't even had time to pray before everything went dark.

But, God, had there been pain. Pain that pulsed and tore inside his body and sat heavy on his chest like cinder blocks so he could only scream in his head. His arms and legs were mired in the quicksand and the pain built and burned inside him until he wondered if he was in hell.

He didn't know how long he spent there—days—weeks—eternity. But he yearned for the one person who soothed his pain like a balm. When she came, her voice cut through the fire in his head, and her touch eased the confusion and fear that crept up on him when the darkness came again. He'd latch on to her words, though he couldn't always understand her, and he'd hold out hope that he'd one day get to see her again.

It was foolish, really. Jade Jax didn't belong to him. She'd never belonged to him. But a man who'd experienced death could be nothing if not honest with himself. He'd loved her from the first moment she and Donovan had been transferred to his team, and he'd been envious of the obvious love between the two of them. He would have hated Donovan just on principle if he hadn't been such a good guy. So he'd been a friend to them both and kept his feelings to himself. It was all he could do.

And then when Donovan died, he hadn't given the job of breaking the news to Jade to someone else. To another female agent or to a doctor or the chaplain. He'd felt he'd needed to do it himself, and his need to be the one to comfort her had cost her everything. She had every right to hate him. But she kept coming back to soothe his pain just when he started to lose hope again.

Then one day the quicksand around his limbs wasn't so heavy and the fire in his head died down to a simmer. And she was there again. Only this time her words were clear.

"Don't die on me, Max," she said, rubbing soothing circles in his palm with her thumb. "You're the best partner I've ever had. Though I wouldn't admit it to Donovan if he were still alive. You know how he liked to try and protect me instead of letting me do my job."

He couldn't say he blamed Donovan for being overly protective. He'd do the same thing in Donovan's position. Warmth covered him like a blanket at the sincerity in her words. She didn't hate him. She wanted him to live. He wanted to squeeze her hand, but his hand wasn't obeying what his mind was telling it. But it was close—so close.

"You're going to miss out on the fun stuff if you stay in here too long. Atticus has big plans for all of us. There are changes coming."

Interesting. And cryptic. Did that mean Atticus had gotten the backing he'd petitioned for? Only a select few of them knew of Atticus

Cameron's plan to open his own security agency and fulfill off-the-books government contracts.

Her hand brushed his hair back from his face, and he wanted to nuzzle against her, to soak in the warmth she brought everywhere she went.

"Just—just don't die on me," she said. "I don't think I could go through it again. I'm not strong enough."

She squeezed his hand and then he knew she was gone because the emptiness made him cold once more. But he didn't return to the blackness he'd been mired in. His thoughts were clear and tingles pricked at his fingers and toes.

He believed in a higher power, and if this wasn't a sign he didn't know what was. Jade was his light. The person who'd brought him back from the brink of death. And she belonged to him. It could take months or years. He didn't care. He'd wait patiently and bide his time. A gift like her wasn't meant to be rushed.

Max felt the heaviness of sleep weigh down on him, but he didn't fear it this time. It was only sleep. And just before he dropped off, he thanked God for giving him a second chance to love Jade.

Three Months Later…

"Come on, Devlin," Jade said. "Ten more reps."

"I'm going to kick your ass if you don't get out of my face," Max said. Sweat soaked his skin and his leg was on fire. He was in a pisser of a mood, but nothing he could say or do would budge Jade.

"You can certainly try," she said, grinning. "But that old guy over there looks like he could take you. You've really let yourself go. Too many Cheetos and *General Hospital* marathons. Eight more reps."

"I know how many more reps I have," he panted. "I can count."

He hated this. Hated that his leg felt as new and uncoordinated as a newborn's. He hated that he had to use a walker or crutches just to go anywhere. At least he was out of the godforsaken wheelchair, but he wasn't much better off. He couldn't drive or go back to work. He was useless.

"I know that look," she said, getting right

into his face. "You're feeling sorry for yourself again."

Max hadn't expected Jade to dedicate herself to seeing him through rehab. They were friends—they'd always been friends—but Donovan had been the glue between them. Or that's what he'd always thought. Maybe he'd tried to keep that barrier between them because she was definitely in the "off limits" category. But loyalty meant something to Jade, and she'd picked him up from his house and driven him to rehab three days a week for the last two months, and she'd stood in front of him yelling encouragement and taunts in equal measures.

Spending so much time with her was heaven—and hell. She'd slimmed down since Donovan's death—her tall frame was lean and muscular—and she had an edge to her that looked dangerous. Her dark skin had lost its healthy glow and she'd cut off all of her beautiful dark hair, so it was short as a boy's and wisped around her face, making her cheekbones more prominent and her face more angular. And her eyes—he'd always been a sucker for those eyes. Brilliant green and a little too lost—a little too sad.

He wanted to hold her—to hug her and take care of her. She'd had much too little of that in her life growing up, and he knew that's why Donovan had been so protective of her. But she didn't need anyone to take care of her. And wouldn't welcome it.

"You're slacking on me, Devlin. If you've got time to daydream then you're not working hard enough."

He leaned forward and took her mouth in a hard kiss before she could say another word. When he pulled back, her eyes had that deer-in-the-headlights stare and her mouth had opened on a gasp.

"Good," he said, nodding. "Looks like I figured out a way to shut you up."

"Why'd you do that?" she asked. Her face paled and she took a step back, running her hand through her short hair with trembling fingers. He felt like a total cad.

"Sorry. It was self-preservation. I thought you'd prefer a kiss instead of my hands around your throat."

Her breath shuddered out with a laugh and she relaxed. "I guess I have been pushing you pretty hard. Maybe we should call it a day."

"I'll finish the stupid reps, woman. I'm not an invalid."

Jade rolled her eyes and Max gritted his teeth. He struggled through the last two reps and let the leg weights drop back to the machine with a clank. He felt a little sick and a lot exhausted. "Finished. Kiss my grits, Jax."

"It's a good thing I know you so well. Someone else might take offense."

She wrapped her arm around his waist and helped him stand and stretch a little. He squeezed her shoulder, silently apologizing for his behavior, and said, "Yeah. I guess it's a good thing. Sorry about the kiss."

"Your technique needs work, Devlin, but I guess it beats being strangled to death."

Max stopped her before she could drag him out to the car. His limbs were shaking with exhaustion and he just wanted to lie down, but he needed to get the words out. "I haven't thanked you for being here for me." What he didn't say was that she'd been there for him when even his own family had been absent over the last months.

"That's what family does, babe."

He couldn't have said it better himself.

There was the family a person couldn't choose, those who shared blood and were obligated to love you because of it. And there was the family who didn't share blood but chose to love you anyway. He much preferred the latter.

Six Months Later…

"Good grief, Devlin," Jade said, clapping her hands over her eyes. "Your neighbors must love you."

It was just past eight in the morning and she'd only planned to drop off the little going-away gift and leave. She hadn't been prepared for Max to answer the door stark naked and angry as a bear. His morning beard was scruffy and glinted with hints of red in the sunlight, and his arm was thrown across his eyes. His chest was broad and ridged with muscle, his waist trim, and a light smattering of white-blond hairs trailed down his flat stomach.

She'd taken in the full sight of him before slamming her eyes closed. Not that having her eyes closed would erase what she'd seen. Her mouth went dry, and something like fear clutched in her belly. She never thought of Max as a man—well, maybe she had a little, but that was only because he'd kissed her and she remembered the heat of his lips against hers and the tingles that had awakened inside her dormant body. He was her friend and he stayed nicely tucked away in that "friend" box.

He grunted something unintelligible at her and went back into the house, leaving the door wide open. Jade followed him in, admiring the back view as only a woman could, and closed the door behind her. She'd have to be dead not to notice, and that was something that had become increasingly clear over the last few months—she wasn't dead. Shame ate at her as thoughts of her husband came to mind and she averted her gaze.

Max's house had always been a little stark, even though it was about ten times the size of her apartment. It was all white walls and neutral colors, light hardwood floors and stainless-steel appliances. A few photographs of the team sat about here and there, but he wasn't one for plants or dust-catching knickknacks other than a signed football that sat in a glass case on his mantel. Boxes were stacked and labeled, and it looked like he was all but ready for the moving company to come load his things.

"I take it the boys decided to send you out in style," she said, breaking the silence.

Max ignored her and walked into the kitchen. It was a big open space, and the only thing that divided it from the living room was the long island counter and the barstools that sat in front of it. He dunked his head into the sink, dousing himself with cold water. He'd let his hair grow longer since the accident, and when he came back up for air it dripped into his face and onto the counter.

Beads of water snaked down his naked chest, and Jade licked her lips, following the trails with her gaze until they disappeared. Her skin flushed. Her mind fought against what her body seemed to want—screamed that she wasn't ready for this—even though she told herself it wouldn't mean anything. It would be mindless sex, and just because her heart was dead didn't mean her body needed to suffer needlessly.

Max dug around blindly in the drawer next to the sink and pulled out a dish towel, drying his face and giving her a look that would have had her shaking in her skin if she'd been anyone else. She crossed her arms over her chest and arched a brow.

"Why the hell do you always have to be so damned chipper at the crack of dawn?" he asked. "It's an unforgivable personality trait."

"That's funny, because I've always thought the fact you can't hold your liquor better than a college freshman was pretty unforgivable."

"I'm sure that's supposed to be funny."

"Maybe you'll feel better if you put on some pants. It's probably not a good thing for every housewife on the street to know you're circumcised." *Please* put on some pants, she prayed. Her control was slipping by the second.

A piratical smile slashed across his face. "It's nice to see you're looking out for me, but no. I'm pretty sure nothing will make me feel better. Not even pants. Though a couple of aspirin couldn't hurt. You could always come back later —when I'm wearing pants—if I'm making you uncomfortable. Or maybe you just like what you see a little too much."

Her lips pressed in a thin line, and she felt her blood surge at the challenge. She knew he was kidding. She was used to banter. Hell, she worked with a team of men, almost all of them ex-military, and she would have left long ago if she hadn't been able to take their colorful vocabulary and trash talk. But this time the banter was too close to the truth.

Wasn't she allowed to need? Donovan was dead, dammit. And no matter how angry she was or how many times she'd gotten down on her knees and begged for his death to be a lie, he wasn't coming back. She was tired of being alone. She was tired of rolling over in a cold bed with no one there beside her. And she was tired of the constant ache inside her soul.

Her emotions warred inside her until she finally found the courage to say to hell with her brain. She wasn't dead. *She wasn't dead*. And Max was safe. She wasn't interested in hooking up with a stranger. It just wasn't part of her makeup to do that. But Max knew her better than anyone, and she knew him.

Max was a sexual creature by nature. He never seemed to be without female attention, and she figured with as many women who had shared his bed that he probably knew what he was doing at this point. She wanted someone who knew how to give her what her body craved and then the ability to walk away with no hard feelings later. It should've been an easy enough task because Max wasn't the type of man to get attached to any woman.

"Maybe you're right," she said.

From the look on Max's face, she could have knocked him over with a feather. Jade stalked her way around the counter and smiled when he took a few steps back.

"I guess it's nice to know it's not one sided," she purred.

"Listen, Jade—" He backed away again when she took another step closer.

"You're the one who made the challenge. I'm just calling you on it."

His jaw clamped shut and she could see the pulse pounding at the side of his neck. His eyes were hooded and the blue of his irises had darkened to the color of a lake in the evening. Jade grabbed the hem of her tank top and slowly lifted it over the top of her head.

"You're making this really difficult," he choked out.

"No." Jade took another step closer, and then another, and Max was effectively trapped with his back to the island. "I'm making this very, very easy."

Her hand reached out and she pressed her palm against his chest. His warmth seeped into her skin and she was suddenly ravenous for more. She was five foot ten in her bare feet, so there was only a few inches' difference in their height. His heart pounded beneath her hand and she leaned up to nip at his chin before fusing her mouth and body to his.

He stood still as a statue for a minute while she kissed him, while she gave him all the pent-up longing and frustration and desire she'd just started to feel again over the last months. And then he was kissing her back and she wanted to shout in triumph.

———

Max's brain deserted him the moment her soft lips touched his. He'd wanted this, dreamed of this for three long years, but even though his dreams seemed to be coming true, he knew this wasn't the way it was supposed to be.

But she was relentless in her pursuit. There was a hunger and desperation inside of her he wanted to soothe. A wildness built inside of him he'd never felt before. She was his mate, and his body recognized her as such, and all he wanted was to possess, to take.

Her lips parted and her tongue licked into his mouth, and the flavor of her exploded through his system. She was sweet to the taste, like sweet cream and melted sugar, and he'd never in his life experienced anything that felt as good as touching her.

"You taste so good," she moaned. "Touch me."

His hands came around her, and he pulled her against him. She groaned into his mouth and he drank in the sound. His tongue dueled with hers and he growled as her fingers threaded through his hair and tugged him closer.

"Please, please," she chanted, and he was helpless to deny her.

His knees were weak and he couldn't seem to find his balance. She was going too fast—racing too hard to the end—and he wanted to take his time now that he finally had her where he wanted her. Their rhythm was off, and he tried to pull back and shake some sense into his head.

Max knew he needed to get control of the

situation because she clearly wasn't. He placed several kisses along her collarbone and then kissed his way up her neck to the lush mouth that had tempted him from the first time he'd seen her. Her top lip was fuller than the bottom and utterly bitable.

"Look at me, baby," he said. Her nails dug into his arms and it was the sweetest pain he'd ever felt.

Her eyes opened and he had to kiss her again. She was stunning. Her face was flushed and there was a glow about her he hadn't seen in much too long. The green of her eyes was vibrant, and she looked like a woman ripe for loving. But he knew her like he knew his own soul, and this wasn't how he'd dreamed of their first time together.

"Don't stop, Max," she cried. "Don't you dare stop."

"I won't be a substitute for anyone else." His breath was labored with his restraint, but he made sure he got his point across. "I've wanted you too long. And if you're coming to my bed it's because you want to be there. Because you want *me*."

She shook her head in confusion and tears

filled her eyes. His heart broke at the sight of her tears and all she'd had to endure, but he couldn't do this. He *wouldn't* do this. He'd waited too long for her to see him as a man. As something other than a friend.

"It's okay if you don't want me," she said, pushing at his chest. "But maybe you could have told me before we got to this point. Now I'll just have to find someone else."

She struggled against him harder as the tears fell, and she swiped at them viciously, but it was like a dam had broken inside of her and nothing was going to stop them from falling.

"Don't make threats, baby. We're past that now."

"It's none of your business, Max. If you don't want it, no big deal. Someone else will."

He clamped a hand on her leg to keep her from running, but she wouldn't look at him. "It is my business. I've wanted you from the first moment I laid eyes on you, but you weren't mine to have. And I haven't waited this long to be some itch you can scratch because you're still grieving for someone else. When you come to my bed, there won't be anyone between us."

A choked sob came from deep inside of her

as she struggled to get up. He released her leg and she bent down and scooped up her shirt from the floor.

"This is your fault, Max," she said, pulling the shirt over her head. She turned and headed for the door as fast as she could. "You're the one who made me feel again, and now you're not man enough to follow through with what you started. Well, to hell with you. Have a nice life in Texas."

He waited until she got to the door and jerked it open before he called out to her. She froze, but didn't turn to face him.

His body throbbed with unfulfilled desire, and his heart felt as if it had been stomped into the ground. But she didn't mean what she said. She wasn't the kind of woman to sleep with just anyone. He knew a part of her had to trust and care for him deeply for her to go as far as she had. But he wanted more. He wanted all of her and he'd meant what he said. He wasn't going to be a substitute for Donovan.

"I've made you feel again," he said. "Remember that it was me when you're alone in that cold apartment. And when you're ready to live for real, you know where to find me."

She didn't look back as she stepped out of his house and his life, and when the door closed with a quiet click, he felt the emptiness of not having her near like a fist to the solar plexus.

"Well, hell," he said. He punched the wall with enough force to leave a dent.

Chapter One

Present Day

"I'm on the roof," Max said. "You've got to be my eyes."

"I've got you in my sights," Eden Kane said through the tiny bud in his ear. "You've got about a minute and a half until the two Secret Service agents make their way back around the house next door. Otherwise you're clear."

"Plenty of time."

His rubber-soled shoes helped him keep traction as he slid down the sharply pitched roof to the small window on the top floor. Black gloves kept his fingers from being torn to shreds, and the black mask over his face and the matching clothes helped him blend in with the night.

The climb up the side of the Dallas mansion had been the hardest part—not to mention a former president lived in the house next door, and on a night like this, when unfamiliar cars and people lined the street, security was at a peak.

The climb had tested his strength and endurance tenfold, and he was glad he'd pushed himself so hard through rehab. Even now, his leg was aching and he'd had to stop for a few seconds to catch his breath once he'd reached the top.

His feet touched on the tiny lip that jutted from the edge of the roof, and he lowered himself down until his hands had a good grasp on the ledge. His muscles bunched and strained and sweat dripped from his temples from the relentless summer heat. He lowered himself inches at a time and then dropped the rest of the way to the balcony. He landed silently and then took the tools from the zippered pocket of his pants.

"Forty-five seconds," Eden said. "I've deactivated the alarms for the top two floors."

"I've got a visual on the senator," Nathan Locke said. "He's dancing with a woman who has a face like a hatchet and a diamond the size of a quail egg on her finger."

Max and Nathan went back to their military days together, and then they'd been recruited in the same class by CIA Director Robert Lockwood. That's where they'd been assigned to Atticus Cameron's black ops team and learned skills normal people couldn't imagine in their wildest dreams. They'd been known by different names back then—Atticus had been known as Reaper, Nate as Warlock, and Max as Zeus. Along with Calvin Cruz and Gabe Brennan—Cypher and Ghost respectively.

What no one knew except for Atticus Cameron, was that Max had been placed as a commander and director of operations at the DEA, all while on assignment from the CIA to infiltrate the United States Department of Justice and dig up the moles who were selling secrets to the cartels. He'd lived a double and triple life for so long he sometimes didn't remember who he worked for, and after Alexander Ramos had shot him and left him for dead, he'd had a serious change of heart about his career choice.

The timing had worked out perfectly because Lockwood had retired from the CIA about the same time their tight-knit unit had started to become disillusioned by some of the assignments their government was sending them on. Gabe Brennan had retired and split off, creating the ISF—International Special Forces—out of London. And Atticus Cameron had created his own private contracting firm—Dynamis Security based out of Dallas, Texas.

Max's only plan after his undercover job with the DEA was finished and he'd left the CIA was to move back home to Texas, buy himself a ranch, and work himself into oblivion while occasionally enjoying a wild Texas sunset. He'd bought the ranch and the house that had come with it, and he'd enjoyed a quiet life. For a while. Until Atticus had shown up on his doorstep after his wife and daughter had been gunned down in cold blood. His daughter had survived—barely—but she was in a coma and he'd had to bury his wife without her knowing her mother was dead.

He hadn't taken any convincing to join

Dynamis Security. Their bond ran deep and true, and Atticus had saved his life. He owed him.

And it was just a bonus he was able to work with his old team. He and Nate had slipped back into their old routine as if they'd never been separated. The only difference was that Nate was now a married man. His wife, Eden, had been Israeli Mossad and she was a good match for his friend.

"The hatchet face would be Martha Sandusky," Max said, taking a slim tool and using it to unlatch the window. "She's the wife of one of Senator Henry's biggest donors." The latch gave and Max slid the window up and slipped inside. "I'm in."

"Just in time," Eden said, her voice soft.

He looked around the small guest bedroom and noticed a few items of clothing and a jewelry case open on the dresser. One of the guests from the party must be staying overnight.

Max stripped off his gloves, pants, and shirt, revealing his tuxedo below, and then he peeled off the thick rubber soles on the bottom of his dress shoes. He carried everything into the bathroom and dumped them in the clothes hamper, knowing a maid would think they belonged to whoever was staying in the room and take them to be laundered. He remembered the ski mask and tossed it in as well.

He checked himself in the mirror, making sure the putty he'd used to disguise himself was still in place. His nose was a little longer and his jaw softer. Dark brown contacts covered his normal blue. He straightened his tie and smoothed back the dark wig. He'd let his own hair grow out since the accident, so it was just long enough to pull into a tail at the nape of his neck, and it covered the ridge of scar tissue in the side of his head quite nicely. But for now it was all tucked under the protective cap. Not even his own family would recognize him.

"The senator is moving to the game room," Nate said. "Looks like he's settling in for a round of poker. Cypher is going to be mad he missed this one. There are almost as many celebrities here as politicians. You know how he likes to stay on top of current events."

"I like to think of it as him being nosy," Eden said. "Besides, he's on his honeymoon. He's not giving work a single thought."

Max grunted and opened the bedroom door,

looking out into the hallway. Music and the muted sounds of laughter could be heard from the first floor, and he quickly left the bedroom and headed toward the back stairway that was reserved for family.

The halls were deserted and he walked boldly through the second floor family wing toward the senator's office. He tested the doorknob and found it locked, so he used the lockpick tools he'd placed in the inside pockets of his jacket.

"Man, I'm good," he said as the lock snicked and the doorknob turned beneath his hand.

"That's not what I've heard." Nate said. "There was a lovely story about you in the *Enquirer* last week. Something about billionaire Lincoln Devlin and his son, Max, who is known as much for his disenchantment with the government as he is for his patriotism. Now he spends most of his time drinking and partying to hide his PTSD and to forget how the government screwed him over in the end. But my favorite part was the women they interviewed. Agent Danger is how Max is known in certain female circles."

"I will kill you, Nate," Max said.

"To think you've wasted that photographic memory on tabloids," Atticus said.

"I've got plenty of room for things besides tabloids," Nate said. "That's just an added bonus."

"And all at my expense," Max said. "I heard you're building shelves for the baby's room. How are those coming along? Have them finished yet?"

"I told you I'd get them done," Nate said.

Eden laughed softly. "I didn't say a word. You're the one who was bragging about your new nail gun."

"So I take it there are no shelves?" Max asked Eden, just to rub salt in the wound.

"Nope," she said, and he could hear the laughter in her voice. "I'm just hoping he gets them built before she gets here. He's still got a few months to deliver."

"That's low, Max," Nate said. "Real low. I was just letting you know how well your cover story was working since you left the agency. You think you know a guy and then he turns on you."

As far as the public knew, Max had involuntarily left a life of service to his country after his almost-fatal injury. To believe the tabloids, the government had screwed him over in more ways than one, so he'd gone back to his wealthy roots like the prodigal son. Though his family had been less than happy to welcome him back into the fold. He'd always been somewhat of a black sheep, and it panged them terribly that his grandfather had left his fortune and stock in the company to Max, on top of his already substantial trust fund.

Being shot in the head by Alexander Ramos was the best thing that could have happened to him—though it hadn't seemed like it at the time. None of his family knew he'd taken a job with Dynamis Security. His family and society thought he was spending his days as a playboy, living off his trust fund and spending as much of his family money as possible on anything from cars to real estate to questionable investments and women.

And yes, the tabloids had started calling him *Agent Danger*—which gave those he worked with unending amusement and ammunition. It didn't matter that he'd never slept with any of the women they'd interviewed or done half the things he'd been accused of. The important thing was that people believed the illusion he presented.

"It's been a while since you and I stepped into the ring," Max said. "I think it's time for a rematch."

"Hell, no," Nate said. "Last time I sparred with you, Eden made me sleep on the couch because she couldn't sleep with all the groans. You have an unfair advantage. I still think you cracked one of my ribs."

"Nah, you're just a girl."

Max did have an unfair advantage in the ring since he'd had MMA training, but Nate made up for the lack of training by fighting dirty. Max had almost as many bruises as Nate, but it had been fun.

He locked the office door behind him and went over to the thin laptop on the desk.

"There's a closed laptop on the desk," he said. "You read me, Eden?"

"I'm here," she said. "I didn't want to interfere with your male bonding time. Go ahead and open it. You'll need to put the device in the USB port, and then I can run it from here."

Max opened up the laptop and watched the

screen flicker on. It was password protected, but Eden could get around that.

Davis Henry was a member of the Senate Defense Committee, and there were enough leaks coming from that office to sink a ship. Too many of America's enemies knew more than they should, and it couldn't be a coincidence any longer. It was a mess the government didn't want to dirty their hands with because Henry held a lot of power, and where there was power, there was money. Always the bottom line when it came to the government. And when the government didn't want to dirty their hands, they called Dynamis Security.

Their mission was to get into the senator's personal files where they suspected he kept records of what he was selling and to whom. As of yet, they hadn't found a money trail, but it would only be a matter of time.

"This champagne is terrible," Nate said. "You'd think they could bring out the good stuff for five thousand dollars a plate."

"It must be terrible to rub elbows with the rich and famous while some of us are sweating our asses off in the car," Eden said.

"Well, when you put it that way—"

"Could we pretend we're on a mission here?" Max interrupted. "Y'all can do marriage counseling later. The device is in the USB. Get me the password, Eden."

Numbers scrambled across the screen before he finished the sentence, and one by one the numbers turned into letters until the password was revealed. The screen went black and then the computer flickered on.

"Go ahead and put the flash drive into the other USB port," Eden said. "We're just going to download his entire hard drive, and then I can sort it all out back at the office on our own computers. He's got several encrypted files that are going to take some time."

"Uh-oh," Nate said. "Looks like the senator had a bad hand. He's headed out of the game room and making his way toward the center stairs."

Max looked up at the door to make sure it was locked and he willed the computer to hurry. He got up and looked around the office. It was bigger than most people's living rooms. Floor-to-ceiling bookshelves were lined up across the wall at his back and a small sitting area sat directly across the room from his massive oak desk. An ugly painting hung on the wall over the sitting area, and it was so obviously a wall safe Max wondered why the senator even bothered to hide it. If he had more time he'd look inside and see if the senator kept hard copies of his records or a journal.

"He's heading up the stairs," Nate said.

Max went back to the computer to check the progress and did a quick search through the desk drawers while he was waiting. His hands were steady and his search methodical.

"Can you stall him?" Max asked.

"Not without jumping over all these people and making a fool out of myself. My other options are to shoot him in the arm or throw a glass of champagne at his head."

"Maybe you should just stay where you are," Max said dryly. He quickly flipped through a stack of loose papers in the top drawer but didn't find anything of consequence. He closed it softly and opened the next drawer. There were still two minutes until the download was complete.

"Wait a minute," Nate said. "It looks like the governor has a bone to pick with Senator Henry. Neither of them looks very happy."

"Not surprising. They hate each other's guts. The governor is a moron but he has impeccable timing. I just need one more minute."

Max finished looking through the drawers and started on the bookshelves. More than one person had the thought that the best hiding places were those in plain sight.

"It looks like the Secretary of Defense needs an urgent word with Henry as well," Nate said. "The governor has walked off in a huff, and now Henry and the secretary are headed back down the stairs in a hurry. Something must be wrong."

"Not our problem," Max said.

"It's clear," Eden said. "You can remove the device and shut down."

"Something's going on down here, Max," Nate said. "You should probably hurry. Some kind of political powwow is happening in one of the alcoves."

"Eden," Max said. "There's no chance our signal was picked up?"

"No, I would have gotten an alert if there was someone else monitoring the system."

Max grunted and shut down the computer, closing the lid and placing it exactly how he'd found it on the senator's desk. He pocketed the flash drive and the nifty device Eden had given him, wiped down the surfaces he'd touched, and headed back to the door.

He listened carefully for anyone out in the hallway and then slowly cracked the door open. The hall was clear and he stepped out of the office and made sure the door locked behind him. He straightened his bow tie and then headed for the stairs.

He almost made it.

"Hey! You there," a man's voice called from behind him. "Stop where you are."

Max turned and gave the guard a superior look. Another guard joined him, and Max swore silently as he saw the guard was already talking into his headset to alert security. Max shoved his hands in his pockets casually and adopted a bored expression, not looking like a man who'd just stolen national security files from the senator's computer.

"Are you talking to me?" he asked.

The guard came closer until he was standing just in front of Max. The stairs leading down to the party on the first floor were more than a dozen feet away.

"The senator's office is off limits to guests."

"I wasn't in the senator's office." Max picked at invisible lint on his sleeve and then gave the guard a sheepish look. "I was in that room right there," he said, pointing to the door next to the office. "A lady friend and I had a—meeting. She's familiar with the house and told me where to meet her. But I'd prefer that not get out. Her husband might not like it."

"You're going to need to come with us, sir," the guard said, pointing toward the way Max had originally come—back to the family wing. "Do you have your invitation?"

Max let out an audible sigh and started walking. He stayed relaxed when the other guard flanked him. "I don't think you know who I am," he said indignantly. "I'm not going to be treated like a common criminal in the senator's home."

Max heard footsteps pounding up the back stairway and knew he had to make his move quickly. His foot lashed out and kicked the guard on his right at the side of the knee. A sickening crack sounded and Max covered the guard's mouth with his hand so his scream couldn't be heard over the party below. Max touched the pressure point in the guard's neck and let him fall unconscious to the ground.

The other guard reached for his weapon, and Max grabbed his wrist, twisting it so the bone broke and the gun fell from his useless grasp. He gave him a short punch to the jaw, and the guard crumpled on top of the other one.

"I need a distraction," he said, running toward the stairs at the front of the house.

"I'm on it," Nate said.

An enormous crash sounded below, and Max heard a few screams from the women in the crowd as champagne glasses filled to the rims crashed to the marble floor and splashed their dresses. Nate had come through, and Senator Henry was apologizing to his guests while berating the poor server Nate had tripped.

Max walked at a sedate pace down the wide center stairs at the front of the house, pushing past the crowd of people that had converged there while they waited for the mess to be cleaned up. He ignored the shouts from upstairs where he'd left the guards and kept moving forward, getting closer to freedom. He reached the bottom of the stairs and Nate bumped against him, giving him the opportunity to slip the flash drive into Nate's pocket. The front door was only steps away and people were starting to panic from the unknown shouts and the sudden swarm of security everywhere.

"There he is!" someone yelled from behind him. "Stop him!" He didn't turn around to see who had said it. His training kicked in, and the only thing he worried about was blending. Making himself invisible. None of the people around him could tell who the guards were pointing to.

"I've got an alternative pickup en route," Eden said. "I just got word from Atticus about half an hour ago that he's in town and we have extra men. I'm trapped behind a limo. Head east toward the next cross street and they'll meet you there."

Indignant shouts of partygoers echoed in his ears as guards shoved their way through the crowd, and Max slipped out the front door and down the garden path. The front gardens were lush and the fragrant scent of roses reminded him of his grandmother—overpowering and slightly stifling. Each of the estates in the exclusive neighborhood sat on a couple of acres that were tree lined and picturesque. Only people with a lot of money could force their lawns to be that green in a Texas summer.

The air was stagnant and smothering and the humidity so thick it felt like breathing water, so the only people outdoors were parking attendants. Max was halfway down the arched driveway before security guards swarmed from each side of the house. He couldn't fight all of them, and he didn't want to kill anyone. They were only doing their jobs. But he knew they wouldn't have any compunction about using their weapons on him, and damned if he felt like taking another bullet anytime soon.

He ran. It was all he could do, and he hoped to God the pickup team was waiting where Eden had said it would be. Yells came from behind him, but he focused on the trees to the east and on the street he knew would be on the opposite side.

The loud crack of a gunshot sounded like it was right next to his ear, and the bark on the tree in front of him exploded, sending tiny shards of wood into his face and neck. Blood ran into his eye and his leg ached as he pushed himself harder and harder. He weaved in and out of the trees, in no particular pattern, making himself a smaller target, but the gunshots didn't stop and if anything, they sounded closer.

He ran out of the cover of trees and straight into the open residential street in front of him. If his driver wasn't there, he was screwed. He heard the squeal of tires before he saw the tiny silver car turn the corner and drive straight toward him. He kept running as the driver's side window opened and a slim hand appeared, holding a semiautomatic handgun.

The driver laid down cover for him, firing shots steadily, and he heard a couple of grunts from too close behind him as the bullets found their target. The driver turned the wheel at the last possible second and the passenger door flung open. Max jumped inside, and the car was speeding back down the street in the direction it had come from before he was able to get the door closed.

"Thanks for the ride," he said.

Jade looked at him out of unreadable green eyes. "It just so happened I was in the neighborhood."

Chapter Two

Max shrugged out of his coat and used it to wipe the blood from his face. None of the cuts were deep, but they were bleeding like a bastard.

"Atticus is going to be pissed," he said. "You know he doesn't like bodies left behind."

"I just winged a couple of them in the leg to slow them down. Everyone's still breathing."

Max winced in sympathy, his own leg aching. He rubbed it absentmindedly to loosen the tight muscle. "They'll be looking for us. We've got to ditch the car."

"Already on it," Jade said.

And weren't they being just so polite with each other, Max thought.

She got onto the highway, weaving in and

out of light traffic, and finally swerved into the far-right lane to take the exit toward the Galleria. Jade's driving had always made him a little lightheaded, but with the pounding headache on top of it, he was hoping he could keep the contents of his stomach down instead of on the floorboard of the car. The mall parking garage was massive and overflowing, and she followed the road as it spiraled upward until they were almost to the top.

Max pushed his hand against the roof so he wouldn't end up in her lap as she took the corners with a squeal of tires. He jerked against the seat belt with an *oomph* as she zipped into a small parking space between two large SUVs.

"You're looking a little pale, Max," she said, her grin letting him know how much she'd enjoyed herself. Her eyes sparkled and there was a flush to her cheeks. This was the Jade he knew. The one he'd met so many years ago who loved what she did and had a zest for life.

"You did that on purpose."

"Of course I did. My driving is the only time I ever get to see you with that look of panic on your face."

"Yeah, well you should have seen me a few

months ago when Agent Carter's wife came to pick him up at the office to go to a doctor's appointment and her water broke right in the lobby. Atticus and I were in the splash zone."

"You're kidding." Her laugh was like music to his ears, and he couldn't remember when he'd heard it last. "Atticus never said a word."

"Because he was just as traumatized as I was. Carter ended up delivering his son before the EMTs could arrive and get her to the hospital. I could go a lifetime without seeing all of that again."

Jade's smile softened. "Well, it's not every day a man gets to deliver his own child. I'm sure Carter knows how lucky he is."

Max could have kicked himself for bringing it up. She hadn't gotten that opportunity with her own husband and child, and he could tell by looking at her that she was remembering that day as he was. But the look of sadness and desperation was no longer so heavy in her expression, and instead there seemed to be a peace that hadn't been there before.

"I've got an extra weapon and ammo in the glove box. We'll need to call in and have someone retrieve the car. It should be fine here for a couple of days though."

Max opened her glove box and removed the extra weapon and magazines she had there, and Jade popped the trunk. He was pretty conspicuous in a bloody tuxedo, and he waited until she'd gathered all of her things before getting out to join her.

"Which one do you want?" he asked, pointing to the line of cars on the opposite side.

"Get the red sporty one."

"How did I know you'd say that?" he sighed.

"Some things never change."

Jade pulled license plates and an electric screwdriver from her bag and went to work while he pulled his iPhone from his pocket. The team had an app specifically designed to override the computers in modern vehicles. The door locks popped open with a click of a button and he slid inside the new model Corvette.

The push-button ignition wouldn't start without a key fob or at least a key fob simulator. He switched apps on his phone and let it scan the computer inside the vehicle they'd picked. It only took a couple of minutes before the phone made the car think it had the right electronic device to start the car. He put his foot on the brake and punched the start button, and the car roared to life. Jade got in the passenger side and he put the car in reverse.

Adrenaline pumped through his body, and he knew when the crash came it would come hard. It had been a little over three years since he'd come close to death, and it had been the hardest three years of his life. He'd changed—inside and out—and even though he was in better shape than he was before his injuries, he still had to deal with the horrific headaches that made him as weak as a baby.

"How's your head?" Jade asked.

"It's fine." Blood dripped into his eye and he swiped at it with his hand as he maneuvered his way out of the garage and back onto the highway.

"Liar. I'm more than happy to drive."

Max just grunted and pressed his foot down on the accelerator. It hadn't really sunk in that she was here sitting beside him. They'd fallen into their old habits and camaraderie as if they'd never been separated, and he felt as if the part of himself that had been missing was finally in place.

It had been more than a year since he'd seen her. He knew she'd gone to work for Atticus as soon as he'd started up the agency. Atticus had a lot of agents who worked for him, but he and Jade had managed to not be assigned to the same missions. Maybe she'd requested it that way. All he knew was she'd done her best to avoid him, to pretend their friendship and partnership had never existed. She hadn't taken his calls or texts so he could apologize. He knew he'd hurt her that last time they'd been together, but two wrongs didn't make a right.

"What are you doing here, Jade?" he asked, more harshly than he normally would have.

He couldn't help it. It hurt that she'd cut him from her life so easily, so completely. And a day didn't go by where he didn't wish he'd somehow handled the situation differently. He could have taken her that day. Given her what her body had needed even though her mind wasn't there yet.

He heard the soft exhalation of her breath. It didn't matter that it felt like jackhammers were pounding away at his skull. That one breath had whispered across his skin until it was everything he could do not to pull over to the side of the road and take her into his arms. He'd missed her.

"I'm here for a couple of reasons," she said. "A problem with your current mission has come to light, and Atticus needs us to try to contain the situation. I'll fill you in once you do something about that headache."

"I told you I'm fine."

"I thought the doctors said the headaches would go away."

"Forgive me for wondering why the hell you care all of a sudden." Maybe he was angrier than he'd thought.

"I guess I deserve that," she said, looking out her window.

"We were friends, Jade. We *are* friends. That above all else. Running away was never the answer."

"I owe you an apology."

"The hell you do," he said. "You've never owed me anything. Did you think I couldn't see you were hurting? That you had needs you'd been ignoring?"

"To tell you the truth, I was embarrassed," she said, looking out the window. "I'm still embarrassed. You always seem to be the one to witness my weak moments, and part of me hates that. I don't want you to think I'm not strong enough to handle whatever comes up."

"Baby, you're one of the strongest people I know. It doesn't make you weak to lean on someone every now and then."

"You deserved better than what I did to you, and all I can say is I'm sorry." She tapped her hand anxiously against her knee and kept checking the side mirror to make sure no one was following them. "If it helps, I've missed seeing your face."

"Yeah, it helps," he said, swiping to clear the blood from his eye again.

Max pulled into the underground parking garage next to the high rise where the Dynamis Security offices were located and parked near the elevators. The gold plaque inside the front of the building said that floors nine to eleven belonged to Reliance Financial Group. It was the same company Atticus used in a similar building in his offices in Washington—a legitimate front for what was really going on behind the doors of Dynamis Security.

His leg buckled when he got out of the car, and he bit off an oath as he had to wait for the muscles to stop seizing before he could walk. Jade kept silent and looked around the parking garage to make sure they were alone, but he could tell she was watching him from the corner of her eye to make sure he was okay.

Max wiped his thumb on his trousers to get the blood off before he could press it to the glowing blue plate next to the electronic keypad by the elevators. His thumb was scanned and the elevator doors opened with a soft whoosh. He could feel Jade's eyes on him while he went through the same procedure to go up to their private floors.

"Tell me about the headaches," she said. "I thought they were supposed to go away after a while."

"They have for the most part." His stomach lurched as the elevator went up, and the pain in his head was so intense blurry spots were appearing in front of his eyes. "It's the adrenaline. The headache is just part of the crash. It's why Atticus hasn't sent me on any missions that will take an extensive period of time. He doesn't want me to be incapacitated in a dangerous situation and have to rely on a team member to get me out. They come on strong and hurt like a bastard, but I'm usually fine if I take something before it gets too bad."

The elevator stopped on the floor to the apartments Atticus kept his agents based out of Dallas—just one level above where the offices were located. There were three apartments at the end of the hall that were furnished but unoccupied in case an agent needed a place to crash or someone needed to be hidden before being sent to a safe house.

His apartment was across from the elevator. The door was oak, but it was reinforced with a steel core that would stop bullets or anything else short of a rocket launcher. He typed in his key code and said his name for the benefit of the voice-recognition program. The door snicked open on silent hinges.

"My apartment is similar to this," Jade said as he flipped on the lights. "The one I have in DC."

He watched as she looked around the open space with approval. The walls were painted a soft ivory and the furniture was leather and overstuffed. Colorful rugs were scattered on the hardwood floor. He wasn't much for decorating, so his walls were bare and his shelves empty except for the worn paperbacks he enjoyed. But it was the view of the city that took her breath away. The windows were tinted so they could see out, but those in the building across the way couldn't see in.

"I didn't realize you'd moved," he said.

"The apartment Donovan and I shared was just a place to land between missions. It wasn't really a home. But the memories there were strong, so I took Atticus up on the offer to move into one of the agency apartments. It was a fresh start. It was the right thing to do."

He didn't know what to say, so he stood there and simply watched her as her hand trailed over the back of the couch. She was beautiful. She'd always been beautiful, but she was one of those women whose looks improved with age. What she'd been three years ago was nothing compared to the woman who stood before him.

Black cargo pants fit her like a second skin, emphasizing the length of her legs, and a black T-shirt was tucked into them. She preferred a thigh holster for her weapon because it fit her better, and for some reason every time she strapped it his desire increased. He'd never stopped loving her, and the pain of the hole she'd left in his heart was still as fresh as it had been the day she'd walked out the door.

"Why are you here?" he asked again.

Max moved into the kitchen, hunting through the cabinet for the bottle of pain pills the doctor had given him for his headaches. He poured out two in his hand and then grabbed a soda from the fridge to wash it down. He tossed one to Jade and she caught it one handed.

She shrugged and popped the top on her soda. "I told you. I'm here because those were my orders."

Max couldn't read the expression on her face. Jade had gotten good at that over the years. She'd been trained as a sniper—to have patience in all things and to think through the best possible outcome. She was quiet in nature and often too serious, but he thought that might have to do with her upbringing as an orphan more than anything. And at the moment, she was closed up tight and nothing he could do or say would get her to tell him the truth until she was damned good and ready.

"The whole team is here and Atticus will

explain everything all at one time," she said. "We've got a mess on our hands."

Max's brows rose and then he winced as the movement pulled at the cut by his eye. "So it took direct orders for you to finally face me?"

"It just sped up the process." She gave a secret half smile. "I would have gotten here eventually. Now go take your shower and I'll tend to the cuts on your face before everyone shows up."

"At some point, Jade, we're going to have a long conversation. I hope to God you're ready for it."

He stalked toward his bedroom, his body trembling with the fading adrenaline and his head pounding so hard he could barely see. He needed her with a ferocity that he'd never experienced before, and it had only grown stronger and wilder since their time apart. She was going to have to tell him exactly what she wanted, without other agendas or needs clouding the issue, because his control was hanging by a thread.

Chapter Three

Jade let out a slow breath when Max headed out of the room. The way he'd been looking at her had been so full of hunger and lust she'd felt the tingles of attraction sliding across her skin. Anyone would be shaking in her boots after seeing a look that hot and full of desire.

She was glad to see Max was a creature of habit when it came to how he lived. The apartment reflected him—solid and comfortable and a little bit dominating. The first-aid kit was under the kitchen sink where he always kept it, and she got everything out and ready on the kitchen table.

She started a pot of coffee for Max—he practically lived on the stuff—and she grabbed another soda for herself. She unstrapped her holster from her thigh and laid it on the countertop—the backup weapon she kept at the small of her back went next to it. More than half an hour had passed before she heard the water shut off.

Feet finally padded against the floor behind her and she smiled as familiarity settled over her. "You've got too much gourmet food in your fridge to fulfill the single man living alone cliché," she said, turning around to tease. But the words died on her lips as she got a good look at him. Her mouth became dry and her heart thudded in her chest.

If his body had been a sculpture when she'd seen it three years ago, it was a masterpiece now. Sweatpants rode low on his hips and a towel was draped around his neck to catch the droplets of water from his hair. He had to have been pushing himself in his workouts because his chest and shoulders were broader, the muscles more defined. And that was saying something, because they'd been pretty spectacular before.

"What can I say? I'm a man who likes to eat."

"Let me look at those cuts." She somehow

managed to get the words past her frozen vocal cords. He sat in one of the hardback chairs, and she could tell by the little half smile on his face he was more than enjoying her reaction to him.

He spread his knees so she could get in close and get a better look at the cuts. The heat of his body felt like a warm blanket and the space between them was so charged with energy it was like she could feel him sliding his hands across her body.

This didn't feel like the last time—when she'd been so desperate—so full of hurt and rage and longing. This time the chemistry wasn't a figment of her imagination. And she had a decision to make. It was obvious he wanted her. He'd said he'd wanted her for years, and she'd never even realized.

He wouldn't have said or done anything while Donovan was still alive because Max was an honorable man, but it amazed her she'd never noticed. Usually a woman could sense when a man was attracted to her, but Max had marked himself as *friend* and had never once crossed the line. She knew this mission was about to change that.

The question was, would they be able to go

back to how things were when it ended? Because there was no doubt in her mind it would end. The Max she knew had never had a long-term relationship. Not to mention with his background and who his family was, he'd eventually need someone who could continue the Devlin legacy and produce an heir. And that person wasn't her.

She'd already made the promise to herself that she would never marry again—never give her heart and soul to one person the way she had with Donovan. That kind of love hurt too much, and she wasn't strong enough to take it again.

"How's your headache?" she asked.

"The medication is kicking in. Though I bet if you kissed me it would work better than the drugs to ease the pain."

She'd spent months wondering if he'd really wanted her as he'd said. Wondering if he'd turned her down because he didn't want to hurt her feelings. Her experience with men wasn't vast. Donovan had been her first and only lover. She wasn't good at reading subtleties or playing the dating game. She was blunt and preferred when others were the same because it was what she understood.

If he'd really been overcome by the sight and feel of her when he'd rejected her before, then he never would have been able to stop. *Would he?* But she couldn't be imagining the interest she saw in his eyes now. She could go into an affair with her eyes wide open this time, without the guilt plaguing her or the anger making her do things she normally wouldn't. This would be a healthy meeting of minds and bodies between two people who knew what they were getting into. And when the mission was over, they could go back to the way things were before she'd screwed them up.

Jade couldn't, and wouldn't, expect anything more from him than a casual affair. Max deserved to have a woman who was whole, who could give him a home and children and hold up the traditions of the Devlin name. She could no longer offer that to any man. Not to mention his grandparents would probably have an apoplexy if he brought home a mixed-race orphan girl from Louisiana. Her future was in her work, and that would have to be enough to fulfill her.

"You've still got some splinters embedded in the skin," she said, touching around the deepest cut near his eye.

She grabbed the tweezers and got to work, taking out the thin slivers of wood as the wounds bled sluggishly. He didn't flinch and he stayed perfectly still, but his gaze never left her face. His eyes were heavy lidded, and the brown contacts were gone so the brilliant blue blazed with hunger.

Warmth spread through her body and it felt as if some invisible thread was binding them closer, though their bodies weren't touching. She stood between his open thighs, basking in his heat and enjoying the feel of him beneath her fingers.

"You said you were here for a couple of reasons." His voice was seductive and low, and she finally found the courage to meet that endless blue gaze. "The first is the mission. But you haven't told me what the second reason was."

"That was careless of me," she whispered.

They stared into each other's eyes, completely lost to anything else around them. It was a stare that lasted too long and saw too much. A stare that heightened the senses and changed how each breath was drawn, so they were completely in sync with one another. It was like being caught in a spell, so body and mind were no longer theirs to command.

Jade drew in a shuddering breath and glanced down at his sensual lips, ripe and full and so tempting she could have spent hours there. But then she remembered he was waiting patiently for her to see to his cuts and heat rushed to her face at how easily she'd been distracted. Only he could do this to her—only when he was near was her ability to focus on the job at hand sorely tested.

The splinters were gone and she wiped the cuts with an antiseptic pad before placing a couple of butterfly bandages over the deeper ones. She froze when she felt his hands on either side of her knees.

"You didn't answer me, Jade. What was the other reason for coming here?"

She couldn't keep herself from touching him, from feeling the coarseness of his stubble beneath her hand. Her thumb skimmed across his bottom lip and his nostrils flared at the boldness of her touch.

"Answer me."

His fingers flexed against her skin with impatience. He reminded her of a big golden tiger locked in a cage, waiting for the opportunity to pounce on whoever opened the door.

"You told me before—" She licked her lips and ran her fingers through his damp hair, massaging the back of his skull. "You told me to come find you when I was ready to live for real."

"And?" he asked.

"It looks like I've found you," she whispered. "Now what are you going to do about it?"

Chapter Four

Jade could see the surprise in his eyes, and the way her challenge affected him. He pulled her closer, so their lips were only a breath apart.

"You're under my skin, Max Devlin. All these years of separation, and I still couldn't get you out of my head. There are no ghosts between us now. Memories—yes. But no ghosts. We're just a man and a woman, and I know what I'm asking for. Give me this one time. Just to make the ache go away."

She kissed him in earnest then, lips and tongues melding. His hand clasped against the back of her head, holding her in place as he took control. If he hadn't been holding her steady, her knees would have buckled because kissing Max was like sending an electrical current through her system.

"You think just once is going to do it?" he asked, pulling away. "You'd better be sure what you're asking me because I promise, the kind of living I have in mind is like nothing you've ever experienced. I want forever."

She shook her head in denial. "I need to be touched. I've missed it so much. Please." Unspeakable pressure was building inside of her. She'd been married and widowed, but never in her life had she felt anything like what was happening to her now.

"I'm going to touch you, sugar. But I know you, Jade Jax, and I see through you. Coming to me is the perfect excuse for you to get what you want and not have to face the consequences. Yes, you're ready to live for real. I can see it when I look at you now. But you're still feeling your way back into the world, and you think I'm a safe choice for testing your wings. You won't use me and cast me aside."

She froze against him as his words mirrored her thoughts. She shook her head to deny him, but the fire burning between them wouldn't be doused so easily.

"Don't push this, Max," she said, her hand pressing against his chest. "I want you. My body comes alive for you. Let it be enough for now." She didn't bother to add he'd probably lose interest before long anyway. She knew exactly what she was getting into. A man like Max could never really love her—not when he discovered the *real* her.

"I've wanted and waited for this too long," he said. "Since I met you, even when I couldn't have you, it's only been you who's haunted my dreams. Once you give yourself to me, you're mine."

She shook her head, denying him the one thing she couldn't give.

"You'll give me everything you have. There won't be any hiding when you're with me. Is that something you'll be able to live with?"

Jade's mind was cloudy with the promises he made, and there was no turning back now—not after she'd come so close to satisfaction.

"I won't be a bystander in this affair," she said. "And I won't be bullied. I may not have as much experience as you when it comes to certain things, but I'm a fast learner and I can hold my own. You may call the shots in the bedroom, but we'll stand side by side when it comes to the job. One has nothing to do with the other. I want your promise on that or I walk out the door right now. Are we clear?"

"Crystal," Max said, smiling. "And don't threaten to walk out my door. Because I'll just hunt you down and bring you back. You're mine, Jade."

And then he kissed her, flooding her senses with the memory of his taste and the texture of his lips. He was intoxicating, and she was already drunk on the promise of what was to come.

She was way out of her league, and as passionate and daring as she'd thought sex with Donovan had been, she realized now how sheltered her experience had been. Not that Donovan hadn't made her blood race, because he had, but the sheer chemistry she felt with Max made her realize how wide the spectrum of pleasure was.

She wished she was the kind of woman who owned sexy lingerie, but she'd never taken the time to learn to be a girl. Her whole life had been about survival, from the time she'd been a child in the orphanage to adulthood when she'd sworn to serve and protect.

But the way Max was looking at her in that moment made her feel very feminine. His eyes were dark with desire and took in every inch of her, as if he were committing the sight of her to his memory.

Her fingers spread across his chest and she'd leaned in to kiss him once more when a sharp knock pounded against the door.

"Of course." Max's jaw clenched and he closed his eyes to get himself under control. "That'll be the team. Atticus always has impeccable timing."

Jade snickered and moved on unsteady legs to lean against the counter and put herself back together. Max looked rakishly disheveled, his hair mussed and his lips swollen from her kisses.

"You look like you've been thoroughly debauched," she said. "If you don't put yourself back together then Nate is going to call you something a lot worse than Agent Danger. You'll never live it down."

"Fine," he said. "You can answer the door and deal with Atticus. He's probably not going to be happy about the way things went tonight. Maybe you can soften him up some."

Jade snorted. "Not likely. There was only one woman who could soften that man up, and it sure as hell isn't me."

Max slipped into the bedroom and she grabbed her weapon from the counter and went to the door—you could never be too careful. She checked the camera and opened the door to the team.

"Sorry to interrupt your party," Atticus said, moving past her and straight to the kitchen. "Some of us would like to get some work done around here."

"Don't mind him," Nate said, following close behind. "You know how antsy he gets when he has to fly. I've never met a man who hates to fly as much as he does, yet has to do it so often."

Nate made himself at home in Max's kitchen and opened the fridge, grabbing a beer for himself and tossing one to Atticus. "I figured we deserve this since things didn't exactly go to plan." Then he looked at Eden. "There's juice or water for you."

Eden rolled her eyes and set her laptop on

the table. Jade didn't know Nate's wife well, but she liked her. And she recognized her skill. Israeli Mossad agents were considered the elite by agencies all over the world.

Eden Kane was an extraordinary woman. Her dark hair was pulled back from her face, showcasing high cheekbones and large dark eyes framed by thick lashes. She was dressed in black and her weapon was still strapped to her thigh.

"I'll take water," Eden said. "Though I'd prefer coffee."

"You'll be up all night," Nate said. "And you drink too much caffeine."

"Which is why I'm drinking water," she said, eyes narrowing.

"She says I hover," Nate said, completely unrepentant. "But she overdoes it if I don't keep an eye on her."

"Women have been having babies a long time," she said, rolling her eyes. "I doubt you've come up with any new advice since the beginning of time. The body knows what to do. Just trust the process."

"Easy for you to say," he said, winking. "Just wait until you can't see your feet and you're asking me to tie your shoes."

"If Eden is anything like Jane was, your opinions are likely to get you kicked in the head the closer she gets to her due date," Atticus said, looking down at his beer as if he'd just realized it was in his hand.

There was an awkward silence as everyone realized it was the first time he'd spoken of his wife since she'd died. Jade knew better than anyone how big of a step that was, and what Atticus must be feeling in that moment. Someone needed to break the silence and the tension, but everyone seemed frozen. And then Max walked into the room.

"Despite the fact that you probably deserve to be kicked in the head," Max said, coming into the room now dressed in jeans and a black T-shirt. "This isn't your first rodeo."

"Yes, but Stella is eighteen and I'm out of practice," Nate said, taking a swig of beer. "I'm older and wiser now. And you're stuck with me, and that includes my hovering. I've got to watch out for my best girl." He winked at Eden and the love between them was so pure and sweet Jade felt the knot in her throat and looked away.

"Maybe we could move on from the mushy stuff and get down to business," Atticus said.

"We've got a firestorm on our hands. Or maybe we should just stop and try to hug it out with the bad guys. Y'all tell me. I'm just in charge."

"I was just asking Jade how she'd gotten pulled into this when you pounded on my door," Max said.

Jade felt the heat in her cheeks before she could stop herself, remembering what they *had* been doing when Atticus had knocked at the door.

———

Max let out a slow breath and ignored the long look Atticus gave him after he watched Jade's reaction to him. Atticus was protective of Jade, just like all of the team was, but Max didn't need the subtle warning he saw in Atticus's gaze. Jade was going to be his. And he'd fight anyone who tried to tell him differently.

He headed to the coffeepot, poured himself a steaming cup, and didn't bother to add cream or sugar. He needed the kick, and he was hoping the caffeine would take the edge off the pain in his head. The pills he'd taken had eased the headache, but the dull throb was still there. At least it was manageable.

"I'd like to know what happened tonight and why Atticus had to come down from his mountain on high," Max said.

"Sometimes I like to mingle with the commoners," Atticus answered dryly.

Atticus took a seat at the head of the table and everyone else grabbed a chair to pull up. He passed out a manila file folder to everyone.

"Senator Henry is screaming from the rooftops about the breach of his security tonight," Atticus said. "Henry doesn't know who broke into his office and tampered with his computer, but he suspects Martin Vassin."

Nate let out a long whistle and Max leaned forward in his chair and said, "I thought Martin Vassin was killed in that explosion at the Kremlin last year."

"Martin needed a little time to regroup after he found himself short of liquid assets when an arms deal went bad with a Turkish terrorist cell," Atticus said. "The weapons were intercepted by the authorities and the Turks were screaming for Martin to make good on his promise by sending someone to enforce the deal.

Martin took the easy way out and chose to die for a little while instead of facing the iron crowbar of the Turkish enforcer."

"So now Vassin is alive and well and his coffers are full?" Max asked. "What's the connection with Senator Henry?"

Atticus leaned back in his chair and steepled his hands across his stomach. Max knew he'd already committed to memory every piece of information that was in the closed file in front of him. Atticus's mind was a machine.

"Vassin is one of the more intelligent arms and information brokers. And he's tapped into Senator Henry. He's got deep pockets and his position on the defense committee is well placed."

"I don't like where I think you're going with this," Max said.

"Wherever you think I'm going just took a hundred-and-eighty-degree turn," Atticus said. "It's a sticky situation. We knew Henry was involved in the high-level security leaks, and this all started about six months ago. Since then we can place the loss of the Iranian military convoy last month and the bombing at the US Consulate in London that killed Senator Ryan at Vassin's feet. Gabe Brennan and his ISF agents are investigating and hunting the parties responsible since Vassin didn't do the dirty work himself. Vassin is just the facilitator."

Max raised his brows at the mention of Gabe Brennan. If both Gabe and Atticus were involved in this, it was big. They'd always been closer than brothers and there was no competition between the agencies. The six of them had been a unit—a deadly force of men who were proud to get the job done and who knew the risks. He could trust his brothers.

"Then Henry's a traitor, plain and simple," Nate said. "And he should pay just like Vassin is going to pay."

"Not so simple." Atticus shook his head. "That's what we found on the flash drive from Henry's personal computer. His nineteen-year-old daughter is a sophomore at Harvard and was studying late one night at the library when Vassin and his men kidnapped her."

"Hell," Max said.

"I started the ball rolling as soon as Eden gave me the information. We don't know where Vassin is keeping her, but he has homes all over the world. My gut says she'll be close though."

"And the senator would do anything to protect his daughter. Even betray his country."

"Bingo," Atticus said.

"Am I to assume you're going to need the Devlin name for this mission?" Max asked.

Atticus's lips twitched. "Why do you think we keep you around? That blue blood comes in handy on occasion. And your cover as the disenchanted agent doesn't hurt either. The word has been put out that you've got sensitive information from your days at the CIA, and that you're willing to part with it for a price."

"Wow, I'm a real jerk," Max said, deadpan.

"This time more than normal," Nate said, making everyone laugh.

"Your mission is to lure Vassin into the open. He never negotiates deals one-on-one. It's how he's stayed alive so long. He'll want to send someone in his stead to make the transaction. You've got to convince him that you'll only work with him directly. We need to take out Vassin and we need to find the senator's daughter. Cal and Evangeline are coming in early from their honeymoon, and Gabe's agents are at our disposal."

"Even his wife?" Nate asked, brow arched.

"I thought she'd turned mercenary, but the last I'd heard he'd brought her back into the fold."

"Gabe says she's back," Atticus said, shrugging. "He knows his people, and I trust him. We're shorthanded on this and need everyone we can get."

"What kind of information am I supposed to have that Vassin will want?" Max asked. "I don't have security clearance anymore."

"No, but you have the drop and destroy locations for all of the confiscated weapons. We have to make it real or Vassin will know it's a setup."

Max raised his brows and ran his hand over the top of his head in agitation. The DEA confiscated ridiculous amounts of contraband weapons in its day-to-day activities. Weapons that not even the military had access to. Arms dealers were more prevalent in the United States than one might think, and the successful ones had a network set up so they could ship contraband weapons all over the world.

Once the DEA got word of a deal and confiscated the shipment, the weapons were taken to a warehouse on one of the military bases where they were highly guarded until the warehouse was full. Then the weapons were taken by convoy to a secured location where they were melted down to scrap. Once the weapons made it to the meltdown location, there was no danger, but the convoy transporting the weapons to the base was vulnerable, even though they were carefully guarded.

"Are you sure?" Max asked. "It could backfire on us if Vassin did happen to get the routes." What Max really meant was that if Vassin somehow captured Max, there was a possibility the location could be tortured from him anyway.

"It'll be fine," Atticus said. "You'll have your bodyguard there as backup. Max Devlin never goes anywhere without a bodyguard. Even the newspapers have remarked on that more than once."

Atticus had started building him a solid cover while he'd been lying unconscious in the hospital, and he'd kept layering on top of it for the three years after. Max was a reckless playboy. A man who skated the line between former hero and current criminal. His friends, associates, and morals were considered questionable. Max was the bad boy everyone in polite society was too afraid of offending. They wouldn't dare turn their backs on him because he wielded too much power over the companies and stockholders that were part of the Devlin fortune.

"And who gets the privilege of standing in the line of fire for me?" Max asked.

"That would be me," Jade said, her lips quirking in a smile. "I am the best shot after all."

"You know, if that wasn't completely true, I'd resent that statement," Nate said.

"I think your ego can take it, big boy," she said.

Nate nodded soberly. "Eden says my ego is very—healthy."

Everyone at the table broke into laughter. Except for Max. He was motionless in his chair, his eyes drilling holes into the side of her head. She'd seen the way his gaze shuttered at the mention of her going in as his bodyguard, and she tried not to let it bother her. But—it did. She was tired of the men in her life trying to stand in front of her all the time. They'd been partners before and he'd never had a problem relying on her. But things had become personal and now there was an issue.

"Max, you and Jade will head down to your ranch tonight," Atticus said. "It won't be long before Vassin gets in contact with you. The rest of us are going to stay here for the time being and keep going through Senator Henry's passcoded files to see if we can find anything else that could lead us to where his daughter is being kept."

Atticus scooted back his chair and stood, tossing his beer bottle in the recycler before heading toward the door. The others all followed suit, and Jade went with them to the door while Max leaned back in the chair on two legs and watched them all.

"Take what you need out of the weapons room with you," Atticus said. "And take the black Explorer in the garage. We'll dispose of the one you lifted earlier. Both of you stay on your guard. Vassin likes to play dirty."

Jade closed the door behind them and turned to face Max, her arms crossing over her chest. "I can tell you right now you're not going to say one word about my assignment," she said. "I saw the look on your face the minute it left

Atticus's mouth. This is my job. And I may sleep with you, but that doesn't give you the right to act like a Neanderthal and make me stand two steps behind you. I mean it, Max. The minute you try to stand in front of me, I walk. Period."

Max's lips thinned in a straight line and he stalked toward her until he stood so close they were almost touching. His arms came up on each side of her shoulders and trapped her against the door. She narrowed her eyes in warning.

"Stop threatening to walk out on me. I know better than anyone how capable you are on the job. But that doesn't mean I can help the natural instincts to try and protect you. I'm a man. I think the Neanderthal is in our genes."

"Some more than others," she said sweetly. "Do you trust me to have your back?"

"Always," he said, with no hesitation. "But that doesn't mean I have to like it. Especially since you *are* going to be sleeping with me. There are certain allowances that have to be made for people you're intimate with."

"Clearly you've been reading Emily Post again."

"Don't be a wiseacre." He leaned down and

gave her a hard kiss, and Jade couldn't help but twine her arms around his neck and kiss him back with everything she had. When he broke away they were both breathing hard and she wondered how soon they had to leave for Max's ranch.

"We'd better not chance it," he whispered, reading her mind. "Atticus will be down here pounding on the door if we're not out of here in the next five minutes."

She laughed, knowing he was right. She felt good. Free. And she realized it had been a long time since it hadn't felt like something was strangling her from the inside. She wasn't weak. And she didn't need to be coddled. Donovan would always have a special place in her heart. He was her first love and the man she hadn't gotten to spend nearly enough time with. The memories would always be there. But time had softened the grief—whether she'd wanted it to or not.

She realized Donovan would've been happy she'd chosen Max. They'd been close as brothers. The last of the guilt that had been wrapped around her heart broke free and a peace settled over her she couldn't explain—as if Donovan were laying a hand on her shoulder and telling her it was okay.

Jade turned away from Max and headed to the door so he wouldn't see the tears in her eyes. She could no longer feel Donovan imprinted on every part of her life. He was no longer her first thought when she woke in the mornings or her last when she went to bed at night. Moving on had happened whether she'd wanted it to or not.

Chapter Five

It was past dawn by the time they got close to Max's ranch, just north of San Antonio in the hill country. The sun was already a bright orange ball rising over the hills in the distance, burning off the thin layer of fog that had settled low across the ground.

The grass along the narrow two-lane road was brown and dead, and the cedar trees were sparse and so dry Jade hoped no one lit a match anywhere in the vicinity. The whole state was liable to go up in flames.

There was a rugged beauty about the whole area—the rolling hills and miles of pastureland—and she could see why Max had been drawn to the area. It was a far cry from his DuPont

Circle brownstone in DC. That posh area of wealth and prestige had belonged to the old Max—the Max who had been more carefree and laughed more easily before his injury—the Max who wore his wealth and privilege like an old cloak.

Jade looked at the man sleeping in the passenger seat, taking in the longer length of his hair and the growth of beard on his cheeks. He overwhelmed the space beside her, and even in sleep, he looked a little bit dangerous—a little bit rough around the edges. Max might have come from privilege, but you couldn't buy your way into the service he'd done for the country. The kind of service that required skills that required training designed to make even the strongest man break down and quit.

He'd worked his way up the ranks the hard way and paid the consequences with a bullet to the head. It was a good thing his head was so hard. Not many men could live to tell the tale of an injury like that. But it had come at a price. There was an edge of danger to him now that hadn't been there before. Gone was the lightness and carefree attitude of the man who'd tried his best to live up to the playboy reputation the tabloids had given him. And she was struggling with the feelings that came from the changes in him. The darkness and danger were very attractive.

She slowed the Explorer as they came to a steep turn and then navigated across a slatted wooden bridge that ran over a creek that was more mud than water.

"We're almost there," Max said, eyes still closed.

"I thought you were asleep."

"I woke up when you started muttering to yourself about the cows blocking the road. You'll get used to it, city girl."

Jade snorted out a laugh. "So speaks the boy with the silver spoons in both fists. I never thought I'd see you living the cowboy life."

Max grinned and stretched, putting his seat back in the upright position. "I've loved every minute of it. Look at all this land. Everywhere you can see is mine. I love getting up before the sun comes up to see to the animals, and I love working my hands bloody with the kind of work that makes your back hurt in the evenings. I love soaking sore muscles in the hot tub and watching the sunset.

"This place was the only reason I considered telling Atticus no when he showed up at my door wanting me to come work for him. But I've got a great foreman and hands to help with the day-to-day operations while I'm away. They all do it much faster and easier than I do anyway. I'm sure it amuses them to have to teach me the ropes, but I've learned a lot."

"I'm sure it helps that you pay well."

He grinned and said, "Yeah, it helps."

"How's the headache?" she asked.

"It's gone. They never last more than a few hours and sleep seems to be the cure more so than the pills. It's mostly an annoyance. Watch the turn here," he said. "The road drops straight off into the ditch."

"I guess you don't get much company out here."

"That's the point. There's no one around for miles and I've got sensors in the road to alert me if someone's coming. I originally put them around the perimeter of the property, but there are so many wild animals they kept setting the sensors off."

Jade took the corner slowly, holding her breath as she kept the Explorer on the narrow road. Max hadn't exaggerated—there was a ten-foot drop-off on each side and the tires came almost to the edge of the pavement. The curve straightened out and she had to squint her eyes against the sudden darkness. Tree branches gnarled over the road and hung low so they almost scraped the top of the car, and limbs scratched against the side windows.

"Good grief, Max. This is a little overboard, don't you think?"

"I like my privacy," he said, shrugging.

"So you're saying I shouldn't have posted the picture of the exit I took on my Facebook page?" She widened her eyes playfully. "Oops."

He laughed. "You're getting a little cheeky in your old age, Jax." His eyes darkened and he reached across the console to trail his finger along her jawline. Things had gone from playful to seduction in a matter of seconds and she was still trying to keep up.

Her breath was tight in her chest as she rounded the last curve and sped toward the house. It was a sprawling single-story house of gray stone and cedar with a slate roof and a wide wraparound porch. There were black rockers and lush ferns. It suited him, she realized.

She stopped the car on the circular drive, and her fists tightened on the wheel. They'd had more time than most to think and wonder about what next steps would look like. She knew Max wanted her and that he was a good man—one of the best men she knew. And their relationship would progress to the next level—an intimate level. It was inevitable.

Her desire for him had only grown over the last three years. Only now she had clarity. It wasn't clouded by grief and anger. She could say with truth that she wanted him—heart, body, and soul. But she also knew a truth that he didn't know and wouldn't understand. There could be no more between them than something physical, and only for a short time. Because the longer they were together, the more a bond had a chance to form, and the more heartbreaking it would be to leave. And she would have to leave. He was a Devlin. And she was a nobody who could give him nothing. What man wanted to be with a woman who couldn't continue his legacy?

"What's wrong?" he asked. "If you're having second thoughts—"

"No, it's not that," she said hurriedly. "To tell you the truth I'm nervous. It's been sexy and fun and banter up to this point, but now we're here and it's just you and me and no interruptions."

His lips twitched. "I'm looking forward to that part."

She couldn't smile so she licked her lips instead. "I just wanted to tell you that it's been a long time for me. I just don't want you to be disappointed."

She could feel his eyes on her, and then before she could turn to meet his gaze he'd opened the car door and jumped out, coming around to her side. He opened the door and then held his hand out for her to take.

"I could never be disappointed," he told her when she placed her hand in his. "Don't you understand, Jade. This is us. And we have all the time in the world to touch and explore and figure each other out. Come to bed with me."

She stumbled as he helped her out of the car. All the time in the world was what she was afraid of.

Chapter Six

Several hours later, the midday sunlight shone through the windows of his bedroom and glanced across Jade's bare skin. Max felt her try to draw away from the arm that encircled her. He somehow found the strength to lift himself so he could see her face. Her eyes were closed and a single tear coursed down her cheek. He couldn't help but wonder if she regretted what they'd just done.

He knew without a doubt nothing in his life would ever be the same. Nothing had ever felt as right as being connected with Jade mind, body, and soul, and he knew he was thirty-six years old and could say he hadn't realized what making love was until just now. It made a difference when you actually loved the person you were with.

He wiped the tear away with his thumb. "Did I hurt you?"

Her tear-drenched eyes opened and she shook her head. "No. You didn't hurt me. I'm just a little overwhelmed. I wasn't expecting it to be so—powerful."

"I'd never ask for you to forget him," he said softly. "He was a good man, and he loved you."

"I know that. I wasn't thinking about him. Not really." She licked her lips in hesitation. "It's just—I feel like I've broken away from that part of my life. Almost as if it never happened."

"Oh baby," he said, touching the side of her face. "Of course it happened. And no one, least of all me, would ever want you to forget what you had with Donovan. But you need to know that I think he'd be proud of the woman you are now. The strength you've shown over the last couple of years. And I think he'd give his blessing that you chose me."

The tears she'd been fighting fell down her cheeks, and he kissed each one away. "And I think if he were talking to me, he'd slap me on the back—God, he had giant hands, didn't he?"

he said, making her smile. "Then he'd warn me that I'd better love you the way you deserved or he'd make me sorry."

Her smile froze and panic shone in her eyes, but he put his finger over her lips when she opened her mouth to speak, halting the denial he knew would come out of them.

"And I'd tell him he didn't need to worry. Because I've always loved you the way you deserved. Even when you belonged to someone else."

Her breath hitched on a sob and she rolled out of his arms until she lay flat on her back. Something felt like it was ripping inside of him. It was obvious she wasn't comfortable with his confession, and he tried to tell himself it was okay. That she probably just needed time. But part of him wondered if she had no deep feelings for him—wondered if he was just someone she felt comfortable with to help her move on to the next stage in her life.

She scrubbed her hands over her face and then sat up on the side of the bed, so her back was to him. "You think maybe we could grab something to eat?" she asked. "I'm starving."

He stayed silent for only a second,

reminding himself to be patient. "Sure. I called the housekeeper before we left Dallas and she should have stocked the kitchen. If you can find something to throw together I'm going to grab a shower." He needed some time to think and lick his wounds.

"What if I can't cook?" she asked, a smile tugging at her mouth.

"I figure if you can calculate the wind and distance when you're firing that rifle of yours, then you can probably follow a simple recipe."

Her laugh was low and husky as she pushed off the bed and grabbed his robe that was hanging on the back of the bathroom door.

"You're taking a hell of a chance," she said as she left him for the kitchen. "I hope you like burnt toast."

He was pretty sure she was kidding.

Jade escaped to the kitchen, pretending she hadn't seen the hurt on Max's face. Her chest was tight and she was finding it difficult to breathe.

What had she been thinking? She wasn't the

kind of person who could enter into a relationship and pretend sex didn't mean anything. All she'd done was complicate things.

She paced around the kitchen, opening the refrigerator and the pantry, noticing the kitchen had been well stocked with all the necessities. She dropped her head against the pantry door and listened intently as the water turned on from the shower.

"Get a grip," she told herself. "You're an adult woman. You've been in life-or-death situations. This is not one of those moments."

She shook her head and decided food could wait. It was time to get solid footing back under her, so she found the guest bathroom and decided to take a shower herself. Maybe it would be easier to face him again if she wasn't breathing in his scent.

When she came back in the kitchen twenty minutes later, still dressed in Max's robe, he was standing in the kitchen in nothing but a pair of sweats. His hair was damp and droplets of water beaded on the back of his neck. His back was to her as he stared into the fridge, but he sensed her presence.

"My kitchen skills are limited," he said. "But

we've got lots of fresh eggs and I saw oatmeal in the pantry. I could probably figure out how to put something edible together."

"I'll make omelets," she said. "You couldn't pay me any amount of money to eat oatmeal." At his confused look she explained. "It's the breakfast staple of orphanages everywhere. Seven days a week, summer, winter, or fall, there'd be a bowl of oatmeal sitting on the table."

"Omelets it is," he agreed.

They worked in companionable silence. She gave him mushrooms and green peppers to chop, while she whisked the eggs. Before long the smell of melted butter and sautéed vegetables filled the air.

"That looks like a little more than a hot tub," she said, looking out the wide kitchen window into the backyard. A large pergola shaded the porch and framed a large rectangular pool with sparkling blue water. A waterfall trickled over the stone that led to a sunken hot tub, and she could see it was the perfect place to sit to watch the sun go down.

"I didn't get around to giving you the full tour. I guess I was in a hurry."

She laughed softly. "Well, your bedroom is very nice. And I love the kitchen."

"It's a big house," he said. "More than I need. At least for now. I had it renovated when I moved in. It's got three bedrooms, two baths, a game room and a living room. Once you've been fed I'll let you pick what room we make love in next."

She couldn't help but laugh at his attempt to get things back on steady ground. They'd been friends first. It was important to remember that.

There was a tablet on the kitchen counter, and Max clicked a few buttons and music played low out of the speakers hidden in the ceiling. Then he set the island with plates while she finished cooking.

"Was it all bad?" he asked, leaning against the counter.

Jade didn't have to ask what he was referring to, though she tried not to dwell on her childhood much.

She shrugged. "It wasn't great." She slid the omelets onto the plates, her mouth watering. "It was the little things that made it difficult. Never having any privacy. Making friends but never getting to keep them. Nothing belonged to you

—not the clothes on your back or the battered schoolbooks that had been donated. It was harder for me because I was almost ten when I went into the system, and I knew what it felt like to be wanted. And then all of a sudden I wasn't."

"I read your file when you were transferred to my unit," Max said. "Atticus and I hand-picked all of my agents. We knew someone was dirty on the inside and I needed a team with impeccable records."

"I didn't know that," she said. Her lips twitched as he got two beers from the fridge. It was an odd combination to say the least.

"Your parents were killed just outside of New Orleans?" he asked.

"Mmm," she murmured, pushing the food around on her plate. She'd never been comfortable talking about her past. Not even with Donovan, but Max just sat there patiently and waited her out.

She sighed. "It was just one of those stupid, senseless things. We were eating lunch at a little restaurant one Sunday afternoon, and some maniac drove his pickup straight through the plate-glass window at the front and opened fire.

My dad shoved me down and behind the table so I was hidden, otherwise I probably would have been killed too."

"And you didn't have any other family to take you in?" he asked.

She snorted out a laugh and shook her head. "Family," she said, knowing the word sounded bitter coming from her lips. "My mother was the only daughter of one of the wealthiest men in New Orleans. Imagine their surprise when she eloped with a poor black law student who was on full scholarship at Tulane. They cut her off without a cent and told her she was as good as dead to them. They didn't even come to her funeral. So they sure as hell didn't offer to save me from the system. And my daddy didn't have any family, so I wasn't left with a lot of choice."

"You turned out to be good people, Jax. Your parents would be proud of what you've become."

"I wonder sometimes," she said. "I wonder if I would have ended up in the same place, doing the same things, if they'd lived."

Max held out his hand and she placed hers on top of it, and then he pulled her to her feet and placed his hands on her hips.

"I like to think you would've ended up exactly where you are." He leaned down and kissed the corner of her mouth. "That no matter where you'd gone or what you'd experienced before, that you'd still end up naked in my kitchen."

"I'm not naked," she whispered.

"Well—" A smile quirked at the corner of his mouth. It was a smile she'd seen frequently from the old Max—the teasing grin and laughing eyes. "My bad."

Chapter Seven

Almost a week passed with nothing more to do than wait, talk, and make love. And Max wasn't afraid to admit a certain amount of frustration where Jade was concerned. At one point during their lovemaking he knew he'd heard her tell him she loved him. That's not something he'd have imagined. But she acted as if she'd never uttered the words, and any attempts to bring it up or talk about possibilities for their future were met with a change of subject or her distracting him with sex.

It was almost as if she didn't believe him when he tried to tell her he loved her and wanted to spend the rest of his life with her. And he knew she was keeping something from him, something that made her afraid of taking the next step, but damned if he could figure out what it was.

The sun was an orange ball of flame high in the sky and temperatures had reached well over a hundred degrees that day. They'd fallen into easy companionship and regular habits through the week—going for a run just before dawn, followed by showers then breakfast. Jade had set up small targets and they'd gotten into a friendly, if very spirited, shooting competition. It stung his pride a little to know she was ahead in points.

Their afternoons had consisted of long, lazy swims and their lovemaking had gotten so creative he was considering taking out extra health insurance. She was a generous and attentive lover, and she was willing to try anything he demanded of her. As long as he didn't try to push the emotional aspect. He almost laughed. He never would have thought he'd be in the position where he was the one who wanted more. He was living every man's fantasy—a dream woman in his bed and no strings attached. Except it was every man's fantasy but his.

"Any word from Atticus?" she asked, stretching lazily on the pool lounger.

"Mmm," he said, appreciating the view as she sunned in nothing but her skin. "Atticus said he's starting to hear rumblings from Vassin's camp. They've been digging deep into both of our files, trying to find something that isn't there. He also said Vassin is putting feelers out, trying to find out how to locate me. This property isn't listed with my other holdings, but it's not impossible to trace. I wanted him to have to work to find me."

"You've never said how your family feels about what you do."

He snorted out a laugh. "I was never their favorite person to begin with. I've always been a bit of a disappointment to them."

Max rubbed the back of his neck, trying to relieve the sudden tension there. He didn't like to talk about his family. His parents weren't the warmest people in the world, and the wound was still deep from the loss of his grandfather in a plane crash. His grandfather was the only person with the Devlin name who knew how to give love and affection.

"I was Grandfather's favorite," he said.

"Especially after I joined the Marines. It gave him a better standing with his constituents to have a grandson in active combat. He also thought it would be good for my record when I was discharged and decided to take my place in politics."

She lifted her head and a smile quirked at the corner of her mouth. "I must have missed that phase of your life."

"Yeah, I missed it too." He felt the tension he carried whenever he talked about his family lighten and was able to laugh a little. "Politics has never been in my purview, but I might have leaned in that direction if Grandad hadn't died. My father decided it was up to him to become the patriarch of the family and tell everyone what to do, so I rebelled at the thought of being forced into that life. My family is very persuasive and they can make things difficult.

"So I took up MMA training while I was overseas to scandalize them, and it became addictive. You can imagine my father's surprise when I signed up to fight in the ring for prize money instead of answering the family summons so I could be announced as the candidate for state representative. He'd planned a big party so he could introduce me to all of his campaign contributors."

"I'm guessing the party was missing something?"

"Yeah," he said. "It was missing me. That's about the same time the I met the Director of the CIA, Robert Lockwood. He said he recognized some things in me that he was looking for to create a specialized team that wouldn't answer to anyone but him. I never looked back after that."

He'd made a lot of detours in his life, searching for something to give him purpose and support as his family never had. Serving his country had given him that purpose, and he was grateful for it.

"Like you, I often wonder if I'd have taken a different path if my grandfather had lived," he said. "It's hard for me to remember him other than what I see from pictures. I remember his laugh and the way he always smelled like peppermint and aftershave. I remember he loved me and reminded me how important it was to bring honor to the Devlin name. To always remember where I came from and be grateful to those before me who'd made sure we never had to worry about where we'd get our next meal."

"He'd be proud of your service," she said. "You've more than brought honor to the Devlin name."

"Not according to my parents. They sent flowers when I was shot, and my father tried to get power of attorney over all my holdings and my trust, using the argument that I'd never be of sound mind again. He's still trying to get control last time I talked to my attorneys."

Jade raised her brows. "On what grounds?"

"Of consorting with nefarious criminals, squandering Devlin money, and blackening the family name. In their eyes, there's nothing in what I've become to be proud of. And I have to let them continue to think that way."

She propped herself up on crossed arms and looked angry on his behalf. That was enough to wash away his own anger at the people he shared blood with. He'd come to realize they didn't have the ability to love or nurture as they should have, and it wasn't worth wasting the time or effort on them any longer, though that didn't make the hurt go away.

"To show you what a good friend I am," she

said, grinning, "The next time you're invited home for dinner, I'm going to let you take me as your date. We'll see what your father has to say about that."

"I'd take you anywhere and be proud of it," he said seriously, watching as the laughter faded from her eyes. "The deficiency is in them, not either of us. Just like it was with your mother's family. Two lost souls." His hand reached out and squeezed hers. "And we turned out just fine."

A high-pitched alarm sounded on his phone and Jade rolled away from him and grabbed the pistol she'd put under the chair. He grabbed his own weapon and the phone and they ran back into the house.

"Someone's on the main road to the house," he said. He pulled on a pair of jeans and a white shirt and then shoved his feet into his boots. Jade did the same thing and then pulled the black bag she'd stashed from under the bed. Max flipped on the flat-screen TV and watched as the surveillance cameras gave faces to their visitors. The road leading to the house made them have to slow down enough that the cameras could see inside the car.

"It's not Vassin," Jade remarked, loading a magazine in her weapon and then putting it at the small of her back. "But there are only two. How do you want to handle it?"

Max picked up his own weapon and then he picked up the familiar thumping sound in the distance.

"Hell," he said.

"They've got a chopper. That could be bad." Nothing much ever fazed Jade. That's why he'd always liked working with her.

Max hit the security panic button and metal shutters closed over all the windows. Damned if he wanted to have to replace a bunch of broken windows if they came out of this alive.

"They'll try to take me," he said. "Vassin wants the information too bad. And these men aren't likely to see you as a threat. Let's let them keep believing that."

"ETA two minutes," she said. "Don't get me wrong. I've enjoyed the week of leisure. But there's something nice about the weight of a rifle on your back."

"Have I told you I'm crazy about you?"

"That's not what you said the time we got

stuck during a hurricane and went three days without electricity."

"That's because I was stuck in close quarters with you and I had to pretend we were just friends. I was going mad."

She winked at him and then chambered a bullet in her weapon, taking her place just to the side of one of the thick cedar posts on the porch.

Max took a seat on the front steps and propped his arms on his knees in a casual pose so no one would get too jumpy, and he watched as a cloud of dust plumed from the bottom of his driveway. A sleek black sedan shot out of the tunnel and sped toward them even as the *whoomp, whoomp, whoomp* from the chopper became louder and the blades kicked up red dust and dead grass.

The helicopter was bullet shaped and black, and it touched down in the wide expanse of his lawn just as the car pulled to a stop. Max slowly got to his feet and walked out to meet the new arrivals halfway. He kept his hands loose at his sides as two men got out of the car.

Dressed in worn jeans and T-shirts, they could have been any average Joe walking down the street. Except for the fact that they looked like thugs. Slicked-back hair and big, meaty hands that would do serious damage if they made contact. One of them had a ragged scar on the side of his eye and the other had a tattoo of a snake wrapped around his neck.

Both of them were armed. Max counted at least three weapons hidden under their clothes. These guys were the muscle—probably hired out locally and too dumb to do any research other than what Vassin spoon-fed them.

It was the two men coming from the helicopter that would have to be watched. They were dressed in black cargos and T-shirts, reflective black sunglasses covering their eyes and their guns visible in the shoulder holsters they wore. They moved with an easy balance that only someone who'd been trained could carry off. They looked ex-military or government, and that just pissed him off.

"You Max Devlin?" one of the thugs from the car asked.

Max ignored him and watched as the two from the helicopter moved in closer. They'd all positioned themselves neatly around him so he stood in the center of their little circle.

"Hey, I'm talking to you," the same guy said.

He could have sworn he saw one of Vassin's personal men grin when he continued not to respond to the overgrown bully. Max kept his gaze on the two in the sunglasses, knowing where the real threat was.

"Martin Vassin requests your presence, Mr. Devlin," Sunglasses #1 said.

"I don't know a Martin Vassin. And I don't have time in my schedule at the moment. You can contact my personal secretary if he's looking for a donation. As you can see, I'm on vacation."

He moved slightly back and to the side, repositioning his body so Sunglasses #2 wasn't at his back, and he nodded to Jade up on the porch. She looked sexy as hell leaning against the porch railing, and the two thugs couldn't seem to take their eyes off her. The two in the sunglasses barely spared her a glance, dismissing her as nonthreatening. Their first mistake.

"I'm afraid we're going to have to insist," Sunglasses #2 said. "You've put out the word that you have something for sale. We'd like to buy."

"Like I said, I don't know Martin Vassin.

I'm picky about my customers and I have a reputation, which you'd know if you bothered to look into my background. Now if you'll excuse me, gentlemen. This is private property."

The guy with the snake tattoo reached out and grabbed his arm and Max gave him a chilling look that had him dropping it in a hurry, though he tried to bluster his way through by taking another step closer.

"You don't want to touch me again," Max said. "It makes my bodyguard unhappy."

"I don't see no bodyguard," Tattoo said. "Just your whore and you, pretty boy."

"What Mr. Evans means," Sunglasses #1 broke in smoothly, "is that Mr. Vassin has given you the option of coming with us the easy or the hard way."

"No," Max said.

No one moved as they waited for him to say something more. But there was nothing else to say. He'd made his position clear.

Tattoo snorted out a laugh. "You can't just say no. He just said you could come the easy or the hard way."

"Yes, Mr. Evans, I can hear. My answer is still no."

A red flush worked its way up Tattoo's face, either in embarrassment or anger; Max didn't know, but probably a little of both. He was the weak link, the one whose anger would get out of control and make him do something stupid.

They all spread out a little around him, widening the circle, and Max smiled, recognizing the brawler in each of them.

"You've messed up, Devlin," Tattoo said, cracking his knuckles. "Looks like you're going to get the hard way. And maybe when we're done with you, Jimmy and I will show your whore what a real man feels like. Maybe we'll let you watch so you can pick up some pointers."

"That's the second time you've insulted my woman," Max said. "You're going to pay for that. And if you do it again, I'll kill you."

"How you plan on doin' that?" the one called Jimmy asked. "It's four against one."

"Well, Jimmy—" Max paused and raised a brow. "You don't mind if I call you Jimmy, do you?" The tension rose higher than the heat and they began to shift, waiting for the opportunity to strike. "The first thing I'm going to do is take out Mr. Evans. I'm going to kick in his knee and then deliver a second kick to the stomach, while using him as a shield so I can take out Sunglasses over here." Max pointed at the man in question. "I'll probably break his arm, but I haven't quite decided yet. I like to keep my options open."

No one moved a muscle as he continued on. "And then I'm going to get to you, Jimmy. You'll want to put some ice on the headache you're going to have. And then that'll leave Sunglasses number two. If he's smart he won't try to throw a punch and I'll let him deliver my message back to Martin Vassin without any damaged body parts."

"You're crazy, is what I think," Jimmy said.

"I've been called worse," Max said. And then he put his words into action. His foot struck out and hit Tattoo's knee, bones and cartilage crunching with a sickening sound, and his high-pitched scream was cut off by the second kick in the stomach.

Max caught him on the way down and used the momentum to push him into Sunglasses #1, throwing him off balance so Max could grab the other man's arm and twist. He felt the shoulder slip out of socket and then he kneed him in the kidney and tossed Tattoo and Sunglasses in a heap on the ground together.

His blood pumped and his muscles sang as he dodged a blow from Jimmy's meaty fist, and the sting in Max's knuckles was sweet satisfaction as he gave Jimmy a quick jab in the stomach followed by an uppercut to the jaw.

The sound of a gunshot had everyone looking up to the porch in surprise. Jade stood much like she had been before, completely relaxed against the thick post, only this time her gun was pointed in their direction, obviously having just been fired.

"No one said knives were allowed in this fight," she said.

Max gave Jimmy another shot to the jaw, taking him down for the count, before he turned his attention to the last man standing. The man's hand was covered in blood and he held his wrist tight where the bullet had gone through. She'd made a hell of a shot—a small target that had been in motion—but he knew she'd hit exactly what she'd aimed for.

A Ka-Bar lay in the dirt at his feet, and Max looked down at his arm, where a long slash oozed blood down his tricep. He hadn't felt the sting with his adrenaline pumping so high, but he was sure he'd feel it soon. At least it wouldn't need stitches.

"I guess you don't get to go back to Mr. Vassin unharmed after all," Max said coolly. Groans came from the men who littered the ground as two of them tried to make their way back to standing positions. Jimmy still lay unconscious. He'd probably be that way for a while.

"Tell Mr. Vassin I expect him to get in touch soon. I won't make deals unless I meet face-to-face. And you can tell him my price has doubled." Max headed back up the porch stairs while Jade kept her weapon trained on the men. "Now get off my lawn."

The two who'd arrived in the helicopter limped their way back and took off for destinations unknown. It took Tattoo a little longer to disappear because he had trouble getting Jimmy into the car with his knee not working properly, but he eventually managed it.

Max didn't slump over and grab his head until they were both out of sight. It never paid for the enemy to see your weakness.

"Come on, tough guy," Jade said, tugging

his arm so it wrapped around her shoulder. "Let's get you a couple of those magic pain pills."

"I guess I should thank you for saving me." His words slurred through the debilitating pain.

"It's just another day at the office," she said. "Besides, I've gotten pretty fond of you."

Chapter Eight

It took less than twenty-four hours for Martin Vassin to make contact and apologize for the "miscommunication" between Max and his men, and then invite Max to Las Vegas to be a guest in his hotel so they could meet face-to-face without the added hostility of other parties. Max had told him he'd need twenty-four hours to decide and had hung up the phone on a very surprised Martin Vassin.

In reality, he'd needed an extra twenty-four hours so Atticus could start putting his backup plans in motion—because Atticus always had backup plans—and so they could gather the necessary equipment and supplies for their trip.

Max's plane was flown into Austin and refueled, and he and Jade had taken off and were almost to Las Vegas before Max called Vassin back and told him they'd be landing in the next ten minutes. He wanted Vassin scrambling and as flustered as he could get him. And Jade was going to help him do that.

"This dress is ridiculous," she said, smoothing down the short black dress she wore. "No bodyguard would wear something this stupid. And how am I supposed to run in these heels? I feel like a giant. We're the same height."

Max's mouth quirked at the continued complaints, and he put his hand possessively on her lower back as they left the plane and made their way to the waiting limo.

"And I've got no place to put my gun."

"I'm sure you'll find some place—creative," he suggested and then helped her into the limo as she struggled to keep her skirt from riding above her waist.

The driver closed the door behind them and they were silent while the luggage was loaded into the trunk. The vehicle finally started moving, and Max waited until they'd turned from the airport onto Wayne Newton Boulevard before he took a device out of his pocket to scan for bugs. He wasn't surprised to find one under each of their seats.

Jade opened her handbag where he knew she'd stashed her weapon, and probably a few other goodies, and she came out with the small rectangular device that would emit the frequencies needed to make the bugs unusable.

"I guess ten minutes wasn't enough time to take him off guard if he's already got listening devices in his limo."

"What do you want to bet they're permanent?" Max said. "He's the type of man who wouldn't trust friends any more than enemies. But you're probably right—I bet they're scrambling to get our room outfitted as we speak."

"What did Atticus have to say? I was putting on this ridiculous getup while you were talking."

It never ceased to amaze Max that the only time he ever saw Jade really uncomfortable was when she had to play a traditional feminine role. She was naturally one of the most beautiful women he'd ever seen—her skin flawless and the bone structure of a queen—but she tried to downplay her looks. She never wore makeup and it was rare he saw her in something other than jeans and T-shirts.

"You're beautiful."

"What?" she asked, flustered by the compliment, and then she tried to joke her way around it. "Atticus called to say I'm beautiful? That doesn't sound like him."

"I just wanted you to know that," he said, ignoring her discomfort. A flush tinged her cheeks and she looked out the window at the passing traffic. "But I think you're beautiful whether you wear something like this or my old robe. And you need to learn to accept a compliment. Just because I tell you you're beautiful doesn't diminish how you do your job. There's no one else I'd rather have at my back. Now say, *thank you, Max*."

Her lips quirked in a half smile. "I don't think so. But if you play your cards right I'll be thanking you profusely later. Now what did Atticus say?"

"They've still got no leads on the girl. He's called in a few favors from a former SEAL team because he doesn't want to leave us without backup if we need it. We've got to keep things rolling with Vassin until they can at least get an idea of where she's being held. Atticus said Vassin hasn't been in touch with Senator Henry in more than two weeks, and the senator is frantic."

Jade bit down on her bottom lip while she thought it out. "It's not good for him to stop communication. It could mean Vassin has reached the end of his use for the senator and his daughter."

"That's what Atticus thought as well. We need to find her fast. Vassin has a home here in Las Vegas. We need to try and get an invitation. Maybe we'll get lucky."

The limo turned onto Sands Drive and then made the slow creep to the massive front entrance of the hotel. It took up the entire block, and towers speared into the sky at each corner while huge angels that had been carved into the sides trumpeted over the street. There was nothing subtle about the elegant veneer—the electric excitement and the undercurrents of desperation could still be felt even in the finest establishments. Max glanced at Jade and caught her surprise as she saw where they were.

"I didn't realize Vassin had done so well for himself. I was expecting a dive off the Strip."

"Illegal arms dealing is a profitable business. And Vassin only owns about thirty percent of the hotel. But word is he's got the capital to snap up more shares when they come available."

He looked Jade over again slowly, and if he didn't know exactly how dangerous she was, he wouldn't be able to tell by looking at her now. She looked softer, and the touch of makeup made her eyes bigger and more alluring. Most of Vassin's men still wouldn't believe she was capable of being a bodyguard, even though the four men who attacked them knew the truth. It wouldn't be long before Vassin learned just how deadly she was.

Jade turned off the white-noise device and put it back in her purse as the limo stopped in front of the hotel, and she pulled down her skirt and wondered how the hell she was supposed to get out of the limo gracefully. It was a lot easier in her opinion to run through the jungle in BDUs than to brave an hour of wearing high heels in polite society. She felt like a fraud any time she had to play the part of sophisticated lover. What did she know? She was an orphan from Nowhere, Louisiana, though she'd worked hard over the years to get rid of any accent that might give her away.

The door opened and she waited until Max got out of the car before she scooted over, and she breathed a sigh of relief that he was thoughtful enough to block the view as he held his hand out to help her.

He didn't try to keep her hand as they followed the bellman into the lobby. Max knew her habits better than anyone, and he'd never tie up her hands in case she needed to get her weapon free. Just like she knew to always stay to his left in case he needed to get to his.

Max broke away as someone in an expensive charcoal suit and red tie met him with an outstretched hand, and she kept watch, looking for signs of Vassin or any of his men in the crowded lobby.

The hotel was too big to see all of the possible hiding places, but she spotted two men in the main lobby who had the look of professionals, though they were both dressed as tourists. She spotted another at the restaurant across the way, sitting at one of the outdoor café-style tables, eating lunch and drinking coffee. He was better at the façade than the others, but the way his eyes kept skimming across the crowd gave him away. That and the bulge she spotted beneath his sport coat.

Jade kept her eyes sharp as the man in the suit led them through a door marked *Private* and then to a wood-paneled elevator that opened with a key card. The suit handed Max an envelope with two identical cards and then they were all rising to the top fast enough to have the bottom drop out of her stomach.

"A lovely room," she said to fill the silence once they were left alone in the penthouse that had been assigned to them.

The main area was wall-to-wall white carpet so thick the heels she wore sank deep into the pile. A long glass dining table that sat ten was on one side of the room and a cardinal-red circular couch like none she'd never seen before sat on the other end. The entire back wall was nothing but glass and looked out over the Strip, but she could see for miles out into the desert beyond.

"I have to say, I prefer the penthouse in my own hotel," Max said, taking the bug sweeper from his pocket and moving from room to room.

"This one is a bit obvious for my tastes. Vassin seems like a man who would overcompensate for certain things in his decorating." He let out a low whistle when he came out of the bedroom. "That bedroom is the perfect example." He waggled his eyebrows. "We'll have fun in there later."

Jade stopped her task of gathering the two tiny listening devices she'd just found in the living area and looked up to see if Max was serious.

"I didn't realize you had a hotel," she said, taking the devices to the table to join the others they'd found.

"Of course I do, love. Seven of them. What kind of self-respecting billionaire doesn't have hotels to diversify his holdings?"

He looked completely serious, and it was sometimes hard to remember that behind the gutter fighter was an honest-to-God businessman. He'd never talked about it while they were at the DEA and most of the other agents they worked with had no idea about his background or that his family was one of the wealthiest in the world. He was just so normal and down to Earth, and she knew he'd be doing the same job he was now whether the money was there or not.

But thoughts of what he'd told her earlier, about how he should always remember where he came from and what the Devlin name stood for, only cemented the idea that she and Max would never work out. She was so out of her league she could only shake her head at the absurdity of it all.

"In fact," he said. "We should take a couple of weeks off and head to Australia. We just opened a new hotel there and I need to check to make sure everything is running smoothly."

Jade watched as Max shook his head at the collection of bugs they'd found throughout the penthouse. More than a dozen sat lined up on the little bar that divided the kitchen and dining room, and she took the neutralizer out of her purse and set it next to them, wondering what to say. Max set the bugs on the floor and then systematically crushed each one beneath his heel before dumping them all in the garbage.

"Why don't we focus on the job here before we start making other plans," she said, nerves prickling along her skin. "One day at a time. I figure you more than anyone else would know that's the best way to live."

"Yes, except for the fact that I happen to love you, even though every time I say it you get that look on your face that you have right now. Is the thought of me loving you that repulsive, or are your feelings for me that nonexistent?"

The words were angry, and the blue of his eyes seemed to become brighter, sharper, as he stared her down and waited for an answer. She'd known this was coming. He'd tried to bring it up on several occasions, and she'd always changed the subject and ignored the hurt she saw in his eyes.

"And how many women have you said those words to?" she asked. "You know what, never mind. I don't want to know. It's none of my business." Her own anger and ineptitude made her lash back at him. "Why can't we just leave things as they are?" She turned away and paced back and forth in front of the bar, while Max stayed completely still. That was never a good sign. Max was always in constant motion.

"I've never said those words to any woman. Not ever. And it pisses me off that even now you don't believe me. I understand if you need time to adjust to what's happening between us, though to tell you the truth it feels like we've been adjusting for years. Yes, I want a future with you and all the things that go with it, but that can wait until you're ready. What I can't understand is that you don't seem to want me to love you at all. Explain that one to me."

"Why the hell aren't you happy that you're getting every man's fantasy? You get to mess around without the nagging and commitment."

His mouth tightened in a straight line and his nostrils flared at how casually she'd debased what had happened between them, and guilt ate at her insides for deceiving him. But she couldn't tell him the truth. Not yet. Though she knew the time would come soon. No one but her and her doctor knew she'd never be able to conceive again. Jade had made sure that secret hadn't gone into any files or reports to Atticus or Max. She didn't need any more of their pity.

And as much as he'd like her to believe that he really did love her, part of her was skeptical. She was a nobody with no background or pedigree, and she had nothing to offer him. Once he got past the sex he'd realize his version of love and hers were two completely different things.

Max's muscles were tense with anger. "So just to be clear." His voice cut like a knife and she would have flinched if she hadn't been holding herself so rigid. "Everything between us up to this point has been nothing but sex. We shouldn't try to cloud the issue with emotions or attachments or talk of the future in general. It's just sex." His voice got softer the more he spoke, which she knew was a dangerous sign. "Just like it would be with any other warm body."

"You're overreacting," she said. "I'm just saying we should enjoy it while it lasts and not dwell on anything else. You're the one trying to make things more complicated."

"Why, because I like to have feelings for the person I'm making love to? I'm not a robot. And we've been through too much together for you to tell me to my face that you don't care for me. Which means there's some other reason for your resistance and you're hiding something from me."

She felt the blood drain from her face, and fear made her words harsh and regretful. "Or maybe you don't know me as well as you like to think you do. Take what you can get, Max. Or you can take nothing. It's your choice."

A knock sounded at the door, but neither of them moved to answer it as they measured each other and where they stood. Jade couldn't take the waves of hurt she felt coming from him, and she finally turned on her heel and headed to the door that led out onto the balcony while Max went to deal with whoever their guest was.

The wind was hot and arid and slapped across her face as she made her way to the half wall that separated her and the three hundred feet to the pavement below. Jade watched the lights and traffic of the city, the movement and flashes of color dizzying at such extreme heights. Despite the heat, her skin was chilled and she wrapped her arms around her torso to ward off the cold.

She heard the patio door open behind her and felt Max's stare.

"That was a messenger delivering an envelope from Martin Vassin. We've got tickets to the heavyweight championship tonight. Front row seats. We're supposed to meet to discuss our options."

"Do you think he'll show?"

"Doubtful. He's playing the watching game for now. He needs time to evaluate what he sees and determine the best way to manipulate us. It's what he's best at." She felt him come up directly behind her, though he didn't touch. She was waiting to see what he'd do with the anger she could still feel lashing at her skin.

"Wear the gold-sequined dress tonight. We don't need to be subtle, and it's best if he doesn't take you seriously."

"Maybe we'll hear from Atticus that they've found the girl and we can take him down without having to jump through his hoops."

"What's the problem, baby? You've already scratched your itch and now you're ready to run back home?" His hands touched her waist and scalded straight through the fabric to her skin.

"That's not fair, Max," she said.

He turned her to face him and she could see the anger banked in his eyes, though his touch was gentle. But then his lips were on hers and she forgot how to breathe. Her fingers dug into his arms and the world spun around her, as if she'd jumped from the balcony in a free fall. She always wanted him. That was her pain and her punishment. Even now, in his anger, she was ready to lie with him willingly.

He pulled away before she could get her

senses back under control. And then she heard the patio door open. "We need to leave in twenty minutes. Be ready."

And then he was gone and she wondered how things had gotten so complicated. Because the only time she'd ever hurt as badly as she did now was when her husband had died.

Chapter Nine

Jade kept her head held high and her expression serene as she and Max were shown to the seats in the VIP section. They hadn't spoken since what had happened between them on the balcony, and Max was doing his best to ignore her, despite his eyes going dark with desire once he saw her in the excuse for a dress he'd asked her to wear.

Gold and sequined, the dress was strapless and fit like a bandage, complementing her skin tone so she looked like a bronzed statue. The dress stopped just above the middle of her thigh and gave the illusion of curves where she knew there were none. Matching stilettos made her legs look a mile long, and she'd actually bothered to put on makeup, so the green of her eyes was vibrant against the smoky shadow and thick eyeliner.

They were close enough to the ring to be spattered with sweat or blood, and she affected a slightly bored expression while she tried to catch sight of Martin Vassin. The arena was packed and the hairs on the back of her neck were standing up.

"I don't have a good feeling," she said, leaning into Max so she could be heard over the noise of the crowd.

"Because you're not an idiot," he said. "We're being watched. I feel like I have a target on the back of my head."

The announcer came on, his deep voice accelerating and growing louder and louder as he introduced the first boxer. The crowd went wild, jumping and screaming, and the whole arena vibrated from the stomps and shouts.

Max stiffened beside her and she looked over to see what was wrong.

"Hey, sugar." Jade arched a brow as a scantily clad ring girl latched on to Max. She read the woman's lips more than hearing the actual words, but the intent was plain as day.

"What do you say you and I get to know each other a little better?" She practically had to yell the words to be heard over the crowd, but Jade saw red as her hand trailed down Max's chest toward his belt. He caught her hand before it could go too low and then quickly let go.

The woman's skirt was white and short and her bikini top barely contained her generous breasts. Her body was tanned and slicked with oil and her dark hair hung in loose curls down her back. Red lips pouted seductively as she moved in closer to Max and slid something into his hand. It was the only thing that kept Jade from knocking her back on her well-padded ass.

There was no doubt she was a beautiful woman, and jealousy reared its ugly head as she wondered again what Max was doing with her. She'd seen some of the women he'd dated over the last few years and she didn't come anywhere close. Jade grabbed the woman's hand before she could rub Max's chest again.

"Don't touch—sugar," Jade said, her smile sharp.

The woman's dark brown eyes flashed once

and then she ignored Jade, turning back to Max while he read the note she'd delivered to him.

"What do you say?" the woman asked, rubbing her breast against his arm. "I've been watching the two of you since you came in. You can't tell me you're together." Her eyes cut to Jade and she smiled cruelly. "Why would you want her when you could have someone like me?"

The question so mirrored Jade's own thoughts she could only stop and wait to see what happened. The woman's fingers walked up Max's chest, and it was Max who grabbed her wandering hand this time.

"She asked you not to touch," he said, his voice dark and dangerous.

"But I promise it'll be worth it," she purred. "Lose the baggage and I'll show you just how much."

Max folded the note and put it in his jacket pocket, and then pulled Jade close so she was snuggled against him. His arm was warm and tight around her, and she let out a breath she hadn't known she'd been holding. She'd missed his touch, and it was only then she realized how distant he'd been.

"Tell Mr. Vassin I'll agree to meet him tomorrow, but if he tries to screw me over again things aren't going to end well." His scowl darkened and the girl took a step back. "Now if you'll excuse us, my companion and I have better things to do. It looks like we were given the cheap seats from where I'm standing."

The girl gasped in outrage at the insult, and Jade couldn't help the twitch of her lips and the small laugh that escaped. Max led her back down the aisle and out of the arena and the crowd. The feeling that someone was still watching them didn't dissipate, and she found herself looking at every face in the crowd as they made their way to the private entrance that led to the penthouse.

As soon as they were in the elevator, Max had her in his arms, his mouth ravaging hers as her stomach flipped from the speedy rise to the top.

"I can't stay away from you," he confessed. "You're like a drug. No matter how much I know I need to keep my distance just to preserve my own sanity, you tempt me back."

Jade tore away from him with a cry, shocked at the pain she heard in his voice.

"What?" he asked. "Isn't this what you wanted? You've gotten your way. I don't seem to be able to go longer than hours without touching you."

"You're angry with me." Her chest was tight, her breathing labored as she tried not to flinch at the coldness in his eyes. "That's not what I wanted. Not how I want things to be between us. You're not thinking about this clearly. Once the haze of sex clears you'll see things differently."

"Do you really think so little of me? That I don't know my own mind and heart well enough to understand what I feel for you?"

"If you do," she said quietly, "Then it's the biggest mistake you'll ever make."

"Only because you're hiding something from me." His anger washed over her and she looked away, willing the elevator to get to the top. "Once you trust me enough to tell me what is going on in your mind, we'll be able to move forward instead of dancing around the real issue. Whatever it is."

The elevator doors opened silently and Max put his hand on her lower back, leading them to the room. He was clouding her mind, making her question her judgment at keeping such a secret from him, and she knew once she told him, the love he spoke of now would cease to exist.

Max held the key card to the door and waited for the green light to come on before they went inside and did another scan. They found two more bugs, neither of which were hidden very well, and Max destroyed them just like he had the first ones. She pulled out the white-noise device and set it on the bar while Max pulled out his phone and made a call.

"Vassin wants to meet at noon tomorrow," he said as soon as Atticus answered the phone. "I need maps for the coordinates he gave me and any possibilities for traps in the surrounding area. Just send them through email." He listed off the coordinates and waited as silence filled the line.

"That's the middle of the desert," Atticus said. "There's nothing around for miles."

"Perfect," Max said, his smile grim. "I've got a plan. Send over whatever you've got on the location. How's the search for the girl?"

"It's like she doesn't exist." The frustration in Atticus's voice was obvious. "Cal was able to trace back the locations of the last emails sent to the senator. We have it narrowed down to a tri-state area, though my gut is going with Vassin's property in northern California. It's a remote area on the cliffs overlooking the water and it's heavily guarded. The SEAL team should be en route tomorrow."

"And where are you?" Max asked.

"In the room directly below yours," he said, making Max smile. "We'll have your back tomorrow."

"Vassin's instructions are for me to go in alone." He caught Jade's eye as he relayed the information to Atticus, and he saw the worry there. "Vassin will be there, but he won't be alone. He'll try to double-cross me."

"What do you have in mind?"

"Let's meet at 08:00. We'll slip down to your room since ours is being monitored so closely. And if things go right no one will die tomorrow."

"Always a good plan," Atticus said and hung up.

Silence and tension filled the room as soon as he put the phone away, and he sighed as exhaustion seeped into his bones.

"Let's go to bed." He held out his hand and waited as she stared at it like it was a trick of some sort. "Just to sleep, Jade. We can table our discussion for another time."

She licked her lips once, the indecision clear on her face, and he dropped his hand.

"I actually thought I'd go ahead and look at the maps Atticus is sending through email," she said. "I think I know what you have in mind, and it'll help to get as much information as possible. The good thing about this place is that the weather is consistent. But I don't want to be taken off guard if I need to make a long shot."

"Good night then," he said, turning toward the bedroom. He stopped when he reached the door and looked back at her. "You know, Jade, I never figured you for a coward."

He didn't wait to see how his words sliced at her. He just stripped out of his tuxedo and hung it in the closet before crawling between the cool sheets of the bed and willing himself to go to sleep. For the first time since his accident he wondered why God had allowed him to survive. He'd thought when he'd first woken in the hospital it was because Jade had given him a reason to live. Now he wasn't so sure.

Chapter Ten

"I think you're out of your mind," Nate said once they were all gathered in Atticus's room the next morning. "You can't think to actually meet Vassin without any backup."

"Tell me how you really feel, Nate. I don't think the rest of the people on this floor heard you."

Cal had manipulated the security feed in the hallway and elevator so he and Jade could sneak down to Atticus's room. The team was already gathered around the breakfast table downing gallons of coffee and looking at the maps he and Jade had already studied until he felt like his eyes would start bleeding. And it seemed like Nate was in a pisser of a mood.

Cal and Evangeline had cut their honeymoon short so they could be at the round table with the rest of the team. Despite the interruption, Max felt a lot better having their help. There was no computer or security system that they couldn't infiltrate, and they were going to make all of their jobs much easier.

"Call me crazy," Nate said. 'But it just seems like a bad idea to go waltzing into enemy territory alone and expect to walk away again."

"There's no other way," Max said patiently. "We're stuck between a rock and hard place until the senator's daughter is located. We have to play out this farce and hope Vassin stays on the hook. As long as he thinks I've got a product to sell, he'll be willing to bite. If we scare him away, he'll probably kill the girl and leave the country. At least for a while. This is the only way we have a chance of getting them both."

Nate paced back and forth in front of the window, his scowl black as irritation came off him in waves. Atticus was sitting completely still, his fingers steepled in front of him, but he had yet to utter a word.

"What's with him?" Max asked Atticus.

"He's usually uptight, but he seems to be in fine form this morning." Max's brows rose in surprise as Nate growled at him.

"Because the doctor called this morning and gave us some news," Eden said, smiling. "Nate's a little overwhelmed at the moment. Apparently the idea of having twins has made him a little crazy."

"Where'd they come from?" Nate asked, exasperated, tossing his hands up.

"I'm assuming they come from the same place just one baby comes from," Atticus said dryly.

"That's not what I mean," Nate said, turning his scowl in Atticus's direction. "I mean neither of us have twins in the family. How are we going to keep up with twins?"

"Sounds like an even match," Max said. "There's two of you and two of them."

"Coming from the man who has no children," Nate said. "And Eden just sits there all calm and beautiful like she has twins all the time."

"Relax, Papa Bear," she said, laughing. "We're a team. We're going to be just fine."

Max felt a pang of jealousy at what Nate had. He knew his love with his wife was secure and would never be thrown back in his face. He'd found a woman who complemented him in every way—a woman who would stand by him no matter what.

"Maybe if we got back to work, it wouldn't worry you so much," Atticus said. He pointed to the area of the map where Vassin had designated as the meeting spot. "There's nothing out here but desert." He looked over at Max, his brows drawn in thought. "We're not going to do you much good if you need fast backup unless we come in by air." Atticus scratched at the scar along his jaw and gave him a steely look out of eerie gray eyes. "The closest cover is more than a mile away in this mountain area, but there aren't any easy roads to get there."

"No," Max said, shaking his head. "You're better off continuing the search for the girl and waiting it out here. Vassin's more than likely going to be pissed after our meeting. If your gut's telling you she's in northern California, then you and the team should head in that direction."

"Yes, because I always leave my agents high

and dry without backup in the middle of a mission."

"That sounded surprisingly like sarcasm," Jade said. "I think he's starting to mellow."

"I can read between the lines as to why you don't want backup from us," Atticus said to Max. "But have you considered all the variables for what you have planned?"

"Yes," Max said. "I don't see another way."

Atticus turned his attention to Jade. "What do you think? The sun could be a problem, depending on where you have to set up."

"The sun will be directly overhead. It'll be fine."

"You know, sometimes it'd be nice for you to actually say whatever the hell you're thinking so the rest of us know what you're talking about," Nate said irritably. "We're not mind readers. That cryptic crap gets old."

"The plan is simple," Atticus said, his smile not at all comforting. "Max is going to meet with Martin Vassin. Alone."

Red sand kicked up from beneath the tires of the Jeep as Max navigated off the main road, following the coordinates that had been mapped out for him. The sun was directly overhead, a red ball of flame that reflected off the sand and made the eyes water with its intensity.

Atticus hadn't been kidding when he'd said there was nothing for miles around. Desert stretched out in all directions, except for the range of mountains in front of him. It took him more than half an hour to reach the designated area, and he wasn't at all surprised to see two black Jeeps similar to his own, and another helicopter. Men lounged against the sides of the vehicles, their weapons visible and dark sunglasses covering their eyes.

Max stopped the Jeep and watched as a man got out of the back seat of one of the vehicles. Martin Vassin wasn't a big man, but he carried himself with an air that only a man who thought he was important could manage to pull off. Despite the hundred-degree temperature, his suit was dark and crisp, and he adjusted his tie before his men gathered at his sides. His hair was dark and silvered at the temples and his complexion was pitted with scars. He was a gangster in a three-thousand-dollar suit. Nothing more, no matter what title he tried to give himself to pretty it up.

Max pulled on his baseball cap and opened the door of the Jeep, letting his feet sink into the sand. His eyes stung, even through the protection of his sunglasses, and already he could feel the grittiness in his teeth.

Vassin's guards took a protective stance as he came closer, and Max almost smiled at their confusion. They wanted him to be afraid, to know who was running the show, and Max wasn't giving them the satisfaction.

Impressions were important to a man like Martin Vassin, and he knew exactly what they saw when they looked at him. They saw a man carelessly dressed in old jeans and a T-shirt with a baseball cap pulled low over his shaggy hair. It didn't matter that Max could've bought and sold Martin Vassin a hundred times. Appearance mattered to him and it was part of his power trip to look more sophisticated, more powerful than his enemy. Max knew exactly how to play him.

"I don't see a suitcase full of money," Max

called out as he stopped about fifteen feet away, drawing his line in the sand.

Vassin's smile was sharp and cruel. "I was under the impression a man such as yourself didn't need my money." His gaze raked Max from head to toe. "Perhaps I was mistaken. Perhaps the rumors are true and you are no longer the one to control the Devlin fortune."

"My fortune is fine. Much larger than yours the last time I checked. This is a business transaction. If you don't have the money, then I don't have the information. It's simple enough." Max turned his back to head back to the Jeep and he felt the movement behind him.

"Just a minute, Mr. Devlin. You don't expect to leave here so easily, do you? I want that information. And I plan to get it."

Hands grabbed the back of his shoulders, and he was spun around to face Vassin again. His men had spread out, and the two restraining him checked him over for weapons before taking a step back.

"He's clean," one of the guards called out.

Vassin's brows rose in surprise. "You're either very brave or very stupid, Mr. Devlin."

"I've been called worse," he said, shrugging.

Vassin chuckled, his eyes filled with curiosity. "This is what we're going to do. You and I are going to get in the helicopter and go to my home. You're going to give me the locations for the weapons convoy, and once you do and the information has been verified, you'll be free to leave. Without my money."

"And if I choose not to go with you?"

"Then I'm going to put a bullet in each of your knees and leave you lying here in the desert. You won't die right away, but the buzzards will still feed off your flesh. I'll come back again tomorrow and see if you've changed your mind about giving me the information."

"Huh," Max said, taking off his cap and running his fingers through his hair. "That's pretty creative of you. But I think I have a better idea."

Vassin's smile grew bigger. "I can't wait to be enlightened. You're an entertaining man, Mr. Devlin."

Max held up the hat in his hand seconds before a shot rang out and a bullet flew right through the center of it. Vassin's men had their weapons up, pointing at Max, but Vassin was smart enough to wave them back.

"The next one is centered to go right through your forehead," Max said. "Your toy soldiers might take me out, but not before you join me. Are we clear?"

Vassin nodded and waved a hand for his men to put their weapons away, and they all did as he asked.

"Now let me tell you what we're going to do. I'm going to walk back to my Jeep and drive away. My price has just doubled again. I expect to see half of the money delivered to a place of my choosing within the next six hours. You'll call me in exactly five hours and fifty minutes for the location. If it's not in my hands in six hours, I'm going to get on a plane and fly to London, where I'm supposed to meet Jarron Sikes. He's very interested in the information I have to offer. And he knows better than to try and screw me over."

Vassin's expression turned deadly at the mention of his closest competitor.

"Once you show your good faith with the first half of the payment, you and I will meet again at a time and place of my choosing, where you'll give the second payment to my associate and I'll relay the information you've purchased."

Max wadded the ball cap in his hands and smiled at Vassin. "Six hours," he repeated. And then he turned around and walked back to the Jeep just like he said he would. He didn't let out the breath he'd been holding until he was back on the main road, speeding toward the city of sin.

Chapter Eleven

It took almost two hours to drive back into the city, and by then Max was starting to get a bad feeling in the pit of his stomach. He hadn't liked the calculating look that had come into Vassin's eyes just before he'd left, and he knew without a doubt Vassin would be thinking of a way he could double-cross Max. Again.

His phone vibrated against the passenger seat, and he picked it up, expecting to hear Jade's voice on the other end of the line.

"I've got a confirmation from the SEAL team," Atticus said. "The girl has been spotted at Vassin's California residence, but we're going to wait to coordinate the rescue with your next meeting. We don't want to take the chance of them killing her."

"He's got less than four hours until the first delivery has to be made, but my gut isn't feeling all that great about the transaction. He's going to try to screw me over."

"Have him make the first drop in a public place. The casino should work nicely for what you have in mind, and the rest of us can spread out to watch for any tricks. We'll already be in place long before he contacts you."

Max's anxiety eased some after he hung up the phone. The ball was in his hands, and it was his show to run. He only wished that one small nagging piece of doubt wasn't eating away at him.

Jade took the mountain pass instead of the desert road that Max had to take so she was back to the hotel long before he was. She changed out of her dusty clothes and got in the shower, scrubbing away the sweat and grime of the afternoon. That hadn't been an easy shot to make, and the conditions up in the mountain where she'd set up had been less than ideal.

She finished showering and dried off quickly, and then she walked with a towel wrapped around her into the bedroom. She still wasn't used to the clothes that had been selected for the trip, and she stood staring into the closet, wondering what she should wear and why the dresses couldn't leave any room for her weapons.

"Wear the red one," Max said from behind her.

She gasped and reached for her weapon out of habit, and then let out a breath of relief when she saw him lounging against the doorframe.

"You're playing a dangerous game," she said, putting her weapon down on the bed.

"I'm definitely willing to play whatever hand you're dealing," he said, arching a brow.

Jade rolled her eyes and then pulled the red strapless dress from the hanger. It had enough elastic in it so she wouldn't have to pull it up every five seconds, but there wasn't a lot of room for error if she bent or sat the wrong way.

And there was no way she would be able to wear a bra.

"With that kind of talk I'm going to let you buy me a steak dinner." Her hair was mostly dry and she combed it down with her fingers so it wasn't sticking up every which way, and she slipped on a pair of flat gold sandals.

He'd already dressed for dinner while she'd been in the shower. He'd changed so much since his injury. The suave and debonair playboy was still there somewhere. You could see it in the way he wore the expensive slacks and shirt, the way his demeanor became almost haughty the more expensive the clothes he wore. But there was a roughness to him now—a wildness that wasn't easily contained—and she wondered if he'd have been the same kind of lover two years ago as he was now.

She was caught up by the sight of him. He was so handsome. So strong and steady. And she loved him. The realization caught her off balance and she had to steady herself. And then the pang to her heart came at what could never be.

"Max," she said. "I want you to know that whatever happens I don't regret anything." She saw his lips tighten and knew she wasn't getting the words out right. That she was messing it up. "I just mean that I'm glad it was you. And that you wanted me."

He came up to where she stood and held out his hand, waiting for her to take it. "I want you like I want to breathe. Never doubt that for a second."

For as long as it lasted, she thought to herself.

Chapter Twelve

It always amazed her how easily she and Max fell into a rhythm outside of work. They knew each other better than most spouses did—quirks and likes and dislikes—because you had to know the person who was watching your six, and you had to trust that they could anticipate your every move.

Dinner was a relaxed affair, and Max delivered on the steak—medium rare and juicy for both of them. They talked about books, because that was one of the biggest things they had in common. It was a love she hadn't been able to share with Donovan because he'd pick a movie any day over a book.

They also talked about their childhoods and

how similar Max's was to her own once she'd gone into the foster system—the disinterest and lack of love his parents had shown—even though he'd grown up in a house with everything at his fingertips. It just went to show that you could be neglected inside the home as much as outside, and from what she could tell, he had no desire to try and mend the rift between them. He'd told her some people just weren't capable of love, and then he'd changed the subject.

Jade could admit she was grateful he didn't try to talk about their future again, or bring up their fight from the day before. He hadn't questioned her again or tried to convince her that he loved her, and she wondered if maybe he regretted the words now, because he was acting like they'd never been said to begin with. She told herself that was a good thing. That the sooner he moved on, the better it would be for both of them, because it was getting harder and harder to convince herself they shouldn't be together—that she shouldn't come clean and take her chances.

Max wasn't a man who would go long without a woman. He was too—primal. Even now, sitting in a public restaurant and obviously with his current lover, he drew the attention of other women like moths to a flame. They gave him long looks and flirtatious smiles, but he acted as if there was no other woman in the room but her. She still didn't understand why he wanted her, but it was very easy for her to understand his appeal.

"Do you think he'll call?" she asked after the dessert dishes had been cleared. It was five minutes until the first delivery was supposed to be made.

"He'll call. He's trying to gain the upper hand again by manipulating my instructions."

They stood and left the restaurant, passing by the expensive shops and the tunnel where an aquarium of sea life swam overhead. The hotel was loud and boisterous, richly gaudy with bright colors and hanging crystal chandeliers. Everyone moved at a frantic pace, as if they'd never get to experience all the delights one hotel could offer them.

Max's hand was a warm comfort on her back as they headed into the casino. The carpets and walls were rich and red, trimmed with gold amplified by the flashing lights of the machines. The clanging of bells, the rush of voices, and the yells of the victorious made her head throb with the need for quiet.

She definitely wasn't a Vegas kind of girl. She liked the quiet, the solitude of her life. Her circle of friends wasn't large, mostly those who worked at the agency, because no one outside understood what it was like to take a life to save countless others. But she was okay with the path she'd chosen because she knew it was a job that had to be done for everyone's sake. And she was good at it.

She caught sight of Nate dressed in cargo shorts and a T-shirt sitting at one of the machines nearby, a bottle of beer at his side as he pushed buttons on the machine. Max led her over to one of the high-stakes blackjack tables and put down enough cash to cover several months of her bills. They were the only ones at the table besides the dealer, and she caught sight of Atticus at one of the poker tables on the opposite side of the room with a big stack of chips in front of him. He was dressed in a tuxedo with the top button unbuttoned and his tie draped around the collar like he'd been on an all-night bender.

She didn't see Eden but she knew she was

around somewhere, and Cal and Evangeline were at the blackjack table to the left of theirs. Evangeline was wearing a white linen sundress and a wedding veil, and every time they were dealt a winning hand Cal pulled her close and kissed her.

At one minute until the deadline, Max's phone vibrated against the green felt of the table.

"You're late," he said into the phone. "You've got one minute to find me in the casino. Otherwise I'm on the next plane out of here to go meet Jarron Sikes."

He hung up the phone without waiting for a reply and finished his hand of cards. Jade watched the second hand click on Max's watch as the minute passed, and then another, and then twenty more. He handed her a stack of chips so she could play too, and he was relaxed beside her, making jokes as her pile grew smaller and his grew larger, but she could tell he was worried that Vassin hadn't taken the bait.

"I'm out of chips," she said almost an hour after Vassin had called.

"Don't worry, you can have more of mine." He gave her one of those slow, lazy smiles that made her heart flip in her chest, and he pushed his chips toward the dealer to cash in. "I guess we should go find something else to occupy our time."

She saw the smirk from the dealer out of the corner of her eye, and she took the hand Max offered her. Atticus and Nate had moved around over the last hour, and she finally caught sight of Jade at the bar, watching a baseball game with seemingly rapt attention. But Jade knew she was aware they were leaving, and she felt Atticus start to circle in closer.

"Stay close," Max whispered in her ear. "Something isn't right."

The problem was going to be when they reached the elevator. Because they were in the penthouse suite their entrance was restricted to regular guests, but Vassin and his men had access to the whole hotel. She caught Atticus's worried gaze and then took a step away and to the left of Max just in case he needed room to maneuver. She had her own instincts, and the only thing she knew was that she had to protect Max, no matter what the cost.

———

Max opened the door that led to the private elevator and saw the long hallway was clear. There wasn't any sound or any sign that someone waited for them, and he and Jade moved quickly to the elevator, their footsteps silenced by the plush carpet. He swiped the key card and the elevator doors whooshed open immediately. He looked inside and saw it was empty before they stepped inside.

Just before the doors closed a man slipped through and had a knife at Jade's throat before Max could move to intercept. He must have been waiting, lurking behind one of the closed doors that lined the hallway. That quickly, things were out of control, and he had no way to get to the man without harming Jade too.

Max's blood turned to ice as he saw the man's hands on her. Her pulse beat rapidly just above where the knife was held, but she was completely still, completely calm. The air felt as if it had been sucked out of the elevator, and Max and the man stared at each other, taking each other's measure.

"You've made a very dangerous enemy, Mr. Devlin," the man said. He was the same height as Jade and he used her body effectively to protect his own. His dark hair was shaved close to the scalp and his beard was the same length. Brown, soulless eyes stared at him, and Max knew he'd slice Jade's throat in a heartbeat and show no remorse if Max didn't tread very carefully.

"I can easily say it's mutual, Mr.—?"

"Smith."

"Yes, very clever. You can tell Mr. Vassin that if she dies then he won't find a corner of the world far enough away to hide in."

The man's eyes narrowed and he tightened his hold around her neck so the blade bit into the skin. A single drop of red welled and Max felt his whole body go still. Dead man walking.

"If he wanted to disappear, you would never find him, but that is not why I am here. We are all businessmen, and Mr. Vassin decided he didn't like the terms you set forth earlier. He felt it was a little one sided. After all, if he gives you half the money, what's to keep you from taking it and leaving him high and dry? Here you go, sweetheart." The man kept his eyes on Max as he put a black briefcase in Jade's hands. "Hand this over to your boyfriend very slowly. I wouldn't want my hand to slip and slice that pretty neck."

Max reached out and took the briefcase from Jade, keeping his eyes on her attacker. He couldn't look at her, afraid of what he'd see in her eyes. Or maybe more afraid of what she'd see in his.

"Be careful, Mr. Smith." He set the briefcase by his feet so his hands would be free. "Good bodyguards are hard to find."

"You seem to be rather careless when it comes to her wellbeing. Do you toss your lovers away so easily then?"

"Well, lovers are easier to find than bodyguards." His casual attitude flustered the man, and he hoped the lack of concentration would be enough for him to make a mistake so Max could strike out. But this man was a professional, and he knew exactly how to hold her, how to position the knife so she'd be dead before Max could ever make a move.

"Why don't you deliver your message so we can get things rolling?" he asked. "I'm a busy man. And I've got a plane to catch. I think I've decided I'd rather do business with Jarron Sikes after all."

"Unfortunately, that is no longer an option. Mr. Vassin doesn't want you to think that he's not an honorable businessman, so the first half of the payment you demanded is in that briefcase. But we're going to take your lover as our own insurance. Once you've given Mr. Vassin the information he wants, you can have her back. An easy transaction."

"And how am I supposed to give Mr. Vassin this information, and where do I reclaim my property?"

"He's extending an invitation to his home here in the valley. Come alone and unarmed. Now hit the button to take you to your room."

Max stared at him out of glacial eyes, and the man must have seen the promise of his death there because he tightened his grip around Jade and took a step back. Max hit the elevator button for the penthouse level and stood impotent while Mr. Smith maintained control.

The doors opened and they stood in silence, still facing each other. "Get out," Mr. Smith said.

Max stepped out of the elevator and into his suite, never turning his back on his enemy.

The doors started to close and Mr. Smith said, "Tonight, Mr. Devlin."

The last thing he saw before the doors closed in his face was Jade staring back at him, with complete trust in her eyes that he'd come for her. And by God, he wasn't going to let her down.

Chapter Thirteen

Max had his phone in his hand dialing Atticus's number as soon as the doors closed, simultaneously taking the frequency device from his pocket and turning it on so no one could hear his conversation.

"What's going on?" Atticus asked. "The staff here watches that private door like hawks. I couldn't get anywhere near it without drawing attention to myself."

"Vassin's man took Jade as collateral and left the first half of the payment with me." Max paused as Atticus swore viciously. "I can meet with Vassin at his home tonight and give him the convoy locations, and then he says I can take Jade and leave."

"They'll try to kill you."

"That's what I'm planning on."

"Give Cal a few minutes to mess with the cameras and then head down to our suite. I've already got blueprints for Vassin's home here. We'll get her back."

"Damned right we will," he said and hung up. His fist punched against the wall and he shook out the sting as he paced back and forth, waiting for the signal that Cal had overtaken the cameras. He changed into sand-colored cargos and a white shirt, and he laced up his combat boots, much preferring their familiar weight over the expensive loafers he'd been wearing.

He didn't have to wait long for Cal's signal, and he took the fire exit down to the floor below his. Atticus was there waiting with the door cracked when he approached their room.

"Vassin lives in northern Las Vegas," Atticus said, closing the door behind him and heading to the table where the maps were spread out. "His home is gated and sits on more than twenty acres of land. We've got an hour until sunset. The darkness will be in our favor. I've got some new toys I've been wanting to try out."

"If he hurts one hair on her head, he's a

dead man," Max said, a vicious fury riding just beneath his skin. "I mean it, Atticus. I don't care what kind of red tape or government promises have been made to hand over Martin Vassin. He will die if she's hurt."

"I'll help you bury the body if it comes to that," Atticus said, nodding. "We're in this together. And you know as well as I do that accidents can happen on a mission. We'll worry about covering our asses when we need to. And if we can't cover our asses then Gabe Brennan can. He owes me a favor."

Max nodded in gratitude and then leaned over the table, staring at the blueprints of Vassin's home. He was so caught up in his plans he didn't realize the phone ringing was his until the sixth ring.

"Devlin," he said, answering the phone.

"So now we are on an even playing field, my friend. This is much better."

Max signaled to Atticus that it was Vassin on the phone, and Cal and Evangeline got to work trying to track his signal.

"Put Jade on the phone," he demanded.

"She's tied up at the moment and unable to

talk. I'm sure you can speak to her once you arrive."

"How do I know she's alive?"

"I guess you'll just have to take my word for it," Vassin said, chuckling. "She is quite a handful. Such spirit she has. And her eyes are like green fire shooting sparks at me. It's very—arousing."

Max's hand gripped the phone tighter and he had to remind himself not to let anger take control. He needed to keep a clear head for Jade's sake.

"I'm assuming there was a point to this call," Max said.

"Ah, yes. Our business transaction. I've decided to play your little time game and see if you're as good at playing by my rules as I was at playing by your rules."

"I hate to break it to you, Martin, but you were pretty bad at following the rules."

He laughed again and Atticus caught Max's eye, telling him to keep him talking while Cal tracked his cell phone. Once he was locked on to it, it would be like a homing beacon once they started looking for him. And once they found Vassin, they'd more than likely find Jade with him.

"Yes, I called your bluff quite handily," Vassin said. "Let me tell you my rules. It is a two-hour drive from the hotel to my home if there's no traffic. You have an hour and fifty-five minutes to get here."

Max paced the floor and kicked at the edge of the sofa. "Or what?" he asked.

"You remember our mutual friend Mr. Smith?" Vassin asked. "He is very good with a knife. You could even say he loves his work. For every minute you're late in getting here, Mr. Smith will start removing body parts. The timer starts now, Mr. Devlin."

The line went dead and he carefully put the phone in his pocket instead of throwing it across the room like he wanted.

"We've got his phone," Atticus said. "He's still en route himself." Atticus handed him an earpiece for communication, and he flicked the tiny sensor to turn it on and then slipped it into his ear. It fit neatly into the canal so it wasn't visible.

Atticus tossed him the keys to his car. "Take mine. It's faster."

Max nodded his thanks. He didn't have even seconds to spare.

"We'll be right behind you," Atticus called out as the rest of the team started gathering their gear. "Try not to piss anyone off too bad before we get there."

Max let the door slam behind him and took the elevator all the way to the garage floor level where Atticus's sleek blue McLaren was parked. The tires squealed as he sped out of the parking garage onto the main street in front of the hotel.

Dusk had already started to fall, and it made the lights of the Strip seem sadder somehow, the people walking the streets with greed in their eyes more pathetic.

He tried not to look at the clock as he sped through downtown and toward the long stretch of highway that would take him to Vassin's home. Night closed in and his foot pressed farther to the floor, taking the car as fast as it could go. He wasn't worried about cops. There was no cop car that could catch him in the McLaren.

The occasional conversation rattled in his earpiece, but he blocked it out once he heard that the team was en route. Atticus always had a little bit of magic up his sleeve. He was always prepared for every eventuality.

He saw the barricade just after he took the last exit off the highway. A car blocked the driveway, and two men leaned against it, waiting for his arrival. He slammed on the brakes and got out of the car almost before it had stopped rolling.

"Not bad," one of the men said, looking at his watch. "You might be able to keep her all in one piece after all. Put your hands on the car and spread your legs."

Max did as he was told, anxious to get a move on. The timer was still ticking. The men patted him down and took the Glock at the small of his back and the Ka-Bar that was in his boot. They cuffed his hands behind his back and then shoved him in the back seat of the black Lincoln they'd been driving, leaving the McLaren in the middle of the road.

He didn't fidget in his seat or try to make his position more comfortable since his hands were behind his back. He just stared into the rearview mirror until the driver kept glancing back at him nervously, and then he finally flicked the mirror up so he couldn't see him at all. Max smiled and looked out the window. They had reason to be nervous.

The car pulled to a stop in front of black iron gates, and they opened slowly, letting the car pass through. Max looked around the grounds for alternate escape routes and then looked at the mansion in front of him. It was three stuccoed stories with white balconies on the top two floors and a terra-cotta tile roof. Palm trees flanked the front walkway and the corners of the house, and a long rectangular pool complete with fountains was the centerpiece of the front yard.

The men pulled him out of the back seat of the car and unlocked his cuffs, and Max flexed his wrists, trying to get the blood circulating again.

"You've got three minutes until they start cutting," the driver said. "But you've got to find them first. Better run."

Max took off through the front door and he heard Atticus in his ear. "The phone signal is on the third floor. West corridor. Last room on the left."

He wasn't expecting it to be easy, so when he took the stairs two at a time to the second floor and met with two of Vassin's goons, he barely paused when they came at him. He was a machine, and his feet and fists were all the weapons he needed. He made short work of the men—a kick to the solar plexus for one and a punch to the jaw for the other—rendering them both unconscious.

He continued up the third flight of stairs and followed Atticus's instructions to where the phone signal had been coming from. He heard footsteps from behind him from the guards who'd just stumbled over their friends, and he took out two more who tried to block his way to Vassin.

When Max burst through the door and into the spacious office, his blood ran cold at the sight that greeted him. Jade was standing against one of the bookshelves, a gag tied around her mouth and her wrists tied in front of her. An apple was precariously balanced on top of her head.

"Ahh, you're just in time for the fun, Mr. Devlin," Vassin said from his place behind his desk. He was leaned back in his chair, his eyes giddy with delight at the upcoming festivities. Mr. Smith stood at the opposite end of the room, tossing a knife in his hand.

Max didn't stop to think. He saw Smith toss the knife one last time and get into position to throw it, and he flung his body at him, taking him down just as the knife left his hand. The rage building inside of him made him feel inhuman, more monster than man, but he didn't hesitate to deliver a killing blow to the throat, crushing his trachea.

He was up on his feet again in only seconds, but killing Mr. Smith had wasted precious time. He looked toward Jade, and his heart almost stopped at the sight of the knife buried in the bookshelf where she'd been standing. She'd dropped to the floor the second Max had moved to attack.

"I'm a gun man myself," Vassin said, pointing the weapon at Jade as she worked at the restraints around her wrists. She'd managed to spit out the gag, and she was working quickly and efficiently to get free.

"You owe me a transaction, Mr. Devlin. I'll take the convoy routes now if you please. And if you even think about lying to me I'll put a bullet through her brain."

Max could hear the commands from Atticus as the team stormed the house. He shouldn't have been surprised that Atticus had brought in extra agents for the job.

"You're going to kill me anyway," Max said. "Why should I give you that location?"

Vassin smiled like he was dealing with a bright student. "You're very astute. It only seems fitting that I kill you since you killed Mr. Smith. I believe you told him that good bodyguards are hard to find. Unfortunately, that's true, and he was mine. Maybe I'll take yours instead. I wouldn't mind a bodyguard that gives bed service. It would certainly simplify things."

Max watched from the corner of his eye as Jade got her hands free, and he moved closer to Vassin, hoping he could get close enough to disarm him. The sounds of fighting echoed in his ear, and he knew if wouldn't be long before Vassin realized something was wrong. And then he'd start taking out whoever was closest.

Even as he had the thought the lights went out and they were thrown into complete darkness. A piercing alarm sounded, and Max immediately hit the ground and began rolling as Vassin started firing into the darkness. His only thought was to get to Jade. He'd pinpointed Vassin's location and was about to pounce when the lights came back on as suddenly as they'd gone off.

It took a second for his eyes to adjust, and that second almost cost him his life. He heard Jade's scream of warning from his left just as Vassin brought the gun up, and he swore the time between when the gunshot sounded and when a hundred-and-thirty-pound dynamo smacked into his side, taking him to the ground with her momentum, happened almost simultaneously.

His arms came around her as they hit the ground, and his biggest fear was that she'd just taken the bullet that had been meant for him. He rolled with her and put her body protectively beneath him as the door was kicked open and more shots were fired. Max didn't bother to watch the red bloom on the front of Vassin's shirt, and he didn't bother to watch as Atticus followed up on his shot with another for insurance.

His hands immediately went to the woman beneath him, checking her body for the bullet hole he knew he'd find. Panic ripped at him, and the rush of blood in his ears drowned out all other noise. But finally he realized she was speaking to him, and that there was no blood.

"This seems like a bad time to cop a feel," she said. "I've never been much of an exhibitionist."

Max dropped his forehead to hers and tried to slow his racing heart. "Don't you ever do that again. You scared the hell out of me."

"Hey," she said, taking his face between her hands and forcing him to look into her eyes. "I was watching your back. That's what partners do. You're one of the good guys. I couldn't let anything happen to you."

"You're one of the good guys too, Jax. But if you ever pull a stunt like that again I'll paddle you."

"Promise, promises," she said.

He was laughing as he kissed her.

"Should we leave?" Nate asked. "I could be wrong, but I don't remember make-out sessions being part of the ops."

"Hey," Atticus said. "My agency has a reputation to uphold. Maybe if you two are finished we can get out of here and call this in for cleanup. The SEAL commander just radioed in and said the senator's daughter is secure. We can debrief later."

"Much later," Max said.

Chapter Fourteen

Jade wasn't surprised to see a very irritated Max standing on her doorstep in DC two days later. They'd flown back to Texas together, but as soon as Atticus had debriefed the team, she'd snuck away like a thief in the night and flown back home with Atticus. She'd been trying to make it a clean break. End of mission. End of their affair.

They didn't have a future together. Max needed someone who could pass on the Devlin name, someone who could give him more than she ever could. And she needed—no, it was best not to think about what she needed. Those answers hurt too badly. She was doing what was best in the long run. Now she just had to make Max understand it.

But him standing right in front of her, looking rumpled and sexy, was more than she could resist.

"You couldn't possibly think I'd just let you go," he said, pushing past her into the apartment.

She let out a little sigh and wondered what to say. What to do. "No, but I had hoped maybe you would. For both our sakes. You're making this too hard, Max. Why do you have to be so stubborn?"

His smile was a vicious slash of white, and she swallowed at the determination she saw there. No, he wasn't going to make this easy.

"I'm a fool in love, and I guess you're just lucky that way."

She didn't try to move away from him as he came closer, his body heat enveloping her like a caress. He touched the side of her face and lowered his head so their foreheads touched. "I thought I'd lost you. Nothing in my life has ever been that terrifying."

She closed her eyes and soaked up the comfort he was offering, touching her hands to his chest to offer her own. "It scared me too," she admitted. "I thought of you. It's what made me fight to get there in time. I wanted to be able to touch you again. To taste you just one more time."

"And yet you ran away," he whispered against her cheek.

"Yes," she said. "Because I had to see if I was strong enough."

"And what did you discover?"

"That when it comes to resisting you I'm very, very weak. Kiss me, Max. Make me feel alive."

His mouth devoured hers in a kiss meant to show them both that they were still living—still breathing. Her hands clasped around his neck and he encircled her in his arms.

"God, I love you," she said almost desperately and then tried to pull away as panic engulfed her.

He froze and then captured her before she could escape his grasp. "Hold on a second. Say it again."

"I can't," she said, shaking her head. "It hurts too much."

"I'll go first," he insisted. "I love you. I heard

you say the words, and you can't take them back. I need to hear them again."

"It's just something people say in the heat of the moment." Her voice caught on a sob, and she wondered if she'd ever be able to forgive herself for lying to him.

"God, Jade. Give me something. Anything. Why are you being so stubborn?" Frustration edged his voice and he ran his fingers through his hair.

"You don't understand!" she cried out.

"Then explain it to me! You've given me your body. You trust me with your life, but not your heart. And you say you love me like it's torture, but you can't look me in the eye and say it now. So yes, explain what the problem is. Explain why I can't get down on my knees and ask you to spend the rest of your life with me. To grow old with me and have children with me."

"I can't have children!" she screamed and then clamped a hand over her mouth as a sob escaped.

Every last bit of air deflated from his lungs as the words penetrated. It felt as if the oxygen had been sucked out of the room. Sound ceased to exist—just an empty void as the blood rushed to his ears.

Reality came crashing back as her gut-wrenching cries broke through the fog surrounding his brain. She crumpled to the floor and curled up in a ball, and her body shook with tremors. To see a woman so strong break down was almost more than he could bear, and he went to her, gathering her in his arms and rocking her back and forth like a child.

"I'm so sorry, baby," he whispered through her sobs. "I'm sorry." He waited until she was quiet in his arms. Until only the occasional tremor shook her body. "I won't ask you if you're sure, even though I didn't see any reports on it after your miscarriage."

She tried to move away from him, but he just shifted their positions so she sat cradled in his lap.

She turned her head away from him when she answered. "I had the doctor leave it out of the written report so I could go back on duty. The damage was too severe, they said. The bleeding too bad. So they had no choice but to give me a hysterectomy or I would have bled to death."

Max let out a slow breath and held her tighter. "I wish you would have told me. You didn't have to go through that alone."

"Maybe I just wanted to delay the inevitable," she said. "I couldn't tell you. At first because I was ashamed of the way I broke down when you told me about Donovan. I'd never lost control like that before." She sucked in a shuddering breath. "And then I lost—I lost the baby, and it was my fault because I lost control."

"No—" His heart ached for her, but she had to know she was wrong. "You can't blame yourself for what happened. It's just as easy to blame myself for the way I told you. But it wasn't anyone's fault, my love."

"Then time started passing and every day it seemed like that day faded a little bit more in my memories, but I still hurt so bad. The grief was overwhelming, suffocating my soul. I kept thinking I could have gotten past the grief if the baby had survived. But I was all alone and there was nothing left of my family."

"Oh, baby," he whispered, and she could feel his tears on her face.

She couldn't seem to stop talking now that she'd started. "And then you were there and I started seeing you as something I never had before. I wanted you too bad to tell you the truth, and at the same time I felt guilty for having feelings like that at all."

Her voice seemed to steady as she explained. "You were right. I think I thought you'd be safe. That you could satisfy my body but not touch my heart because I didn't believe I'd ever be able to love again. And I didn't think that you could ever love me. I've watched the women go in and out of your life over the years, and I thought I could be one of them, and that you'd make me feel something again. I was devastated and embarrassed when you rejected me. But I'd had a taste of you, and it was all I could think about—dream about.

"We'd already had years of friendship and connection. And that first time we made love—" She hesitated, her breath hitching. "I realized that I was lying to myself and I loved you more than I thought I would ever be capable of loving again."

"Jade—" He kissed her brow and pulled her closer. "I loved you when you belonged to someone else, and I love you even more now that you're mine. And there will be no more women in and out of my life. In fact, there hasn't been any woman but you in my bed since you walked out of my kitchen. I knew after one taste that you were it for me."

"That's what I was afraid of," she said. "You deserve so much more than what I can give you, Max. You deserve to have a woman who's whole, so you can get down on your knees and ask her to spend her life with you. To have children with you."

"You're going to piss me off, love," he said, rubbing his thumb along her bottom lip. "Do you think you telling me you can't have children is going to make me stop loving you? Let me ask you something," he said before she could answer. "When you were stuck inside that orphanage, did you dream of a couple like us coming in to take you home? Do you think there's not someone exactly like you waiting for us right now? Or that there won't be two or five or ten years from now? You make me whole, Jade. Just you. Not anything else. As long as I have you then everything else will happen as it should."

"You make it sound so simple." She

scrubbed her hands over her face, wiping away the tears.

"Because it is simple," he said. "Marry me. Love me. And let me love you back. Nothing else matters."

"Your family might have something to say about that," she said with a bitter laugh. "You can trace the Devlin name practically to the dawn of time. You have a legacy, Max. Something you can only pass down to a biological child. Why would you deny yourself that?"

"I can just as easily pass it to a child who needs a good home," he said with a shrug. "They're just things, Jade. It's just a name. It pales in comparison to spending the rest of my life without you."

Her arms wrapped around him and she buried her face against his chest. "I love you so much," she whispered.

"That's a step in the right direction for sure. I'm not on my knees, but I'm pretty close," he said, lifting her face once more and seeing the hope in her eyes. "Marry me, Jade. Spend your life with me. Love me."

"I love you more than you know," she said. "Always."

Epilogue

Two Months Later...

The bride was beautiful. It was all Max could think as he watched her walk down the aisle, the white gown showing off the glow of her skin and the radiance in her eyes.

The wedding was held at his ranch, under a canopy of trees burnished red and orange and gold as summer finally gave way to fall. Nate stood as his best man. And then Atticus, Cal and Gabe Brennan, who'd come in from London for the occasion, stood next to Nate. Max looked out at those witnessing their special day with pride. All the family he needed was here to watch him take Jade as his wife.

The smile she gave him as she met him at

the end of the aisle had his heart swelling in his chest. Love shone across her whole face and there was a joy inside her he hadn't seen in a long time. She took his outstretched hand, and it was easy to see their future in her eyes as they promised to love and cherish for a lifetime.

And at the end of the ceremony, Max closed his eyes and said a small prayer, thanking Donovan for being there to love her first. To love her how she deserved. And then he thanked him for giving Max the gift of being able to love her too.

Gabe Brennan is mentioned several times in the Dynamis Security Series as one of the original team members, also known as Ghost. Check out his story in The Lies We Tell. Now available at all retailers!

By her calculations, Grace Meredith had exactly five and a half seconds to take out six targets before an alarm sounded. She had a round in the chamber and five in the magazine of her M40A5. Piece of cake.

She ignored the mosquitoes the size of hummingbirds searching for exposed flesh, and she disregarded the sweat that dripped steadily down her spine as she looked through the scope of her rifle. The temperature was in the mid-nineties, but the canopy of trees that blanketed the area held the heat in like an oven and slowly baked anyone who didn't have shelter with a running AC. Her body and mind were disciplined, so the discomforts barely registered.

Colombia wasn't known for its gentle climate. Or gentle anything for that matter. Gemino Vasquez was Colombia's baddest arms dealer, and lately his biggest client had been North Korea. But Vasquez had something Grace wanted very badly. Something that would bring in a big, fat paycheck from the South Korean government.

She shifted slightly, and the bark of the large tree branch she'd lain on for the last four hours ground against her stomach. But her focus was absolute. Not even the hundred-and-fifty-foot drop to the ground could distract her.

The orange sun blazed just over the tops of the trees, but it would disappear completely in another twenty minutes. By the time it was gone, she'd have the flash drive in hand and already be across the border to Venezuela.

Grace did one final check of all her equipment and took a deep, steadying breath, slowing her heartbeat so her pulse would be in time with-b each shot. She'd hit the sentry at the top of the Vasquez compound first and then take the rest in order from left to right. She pushed her feet against the tree for balance. The clock ticked in the background of her mind as she put the slightest amount of pressure on the trigger.

"One," she whispered. She didn't wait to watch him fall but moved to the next target. Five seconds until the report from her rifle reached their ears. Five seconds for five more kills.

Two…
Three…
Four…
Five…
Six…

Grace didn't stop to check the accuracy of her shots. She never missed a target. She hung her rifle on a tree branch, already missing the feel of it in her hands. Time was of the essence now, and she couldn't afford to be burdened with too much equipment—she'd have to leave it behind. The new guards would be driving up soon for the shift change, and she had to be long gone by then.

She unzipped her supply pack, pulling out a lightweight pipe no longer than her forearm. It looked completely worthless at first glance. In reality, it was a military prototype she'd borrowed from her former life. She hit the button on each end of the pipe and it expanded in length until it was almost as tall as she was, and then she hit the button in the center and waited as wings made out of a synthetic material unfurled to complete the hang glider.

Excerpt of The Lies We Tell

"No time like the present," she said, swallowing as she perched on the edge of the tree and looked out across the jungle. She had a straight shot into the compound, but any shift in wind would have her hurtling into trees. Falling to her death wouldn't bring her the money she needed, so she had no choice but to take a leap of faith. Literally.

Fifteen minutes until all hell breaks loose.

Grace grasped the bar and jumped. The bottom dropped out of her stomach as she free-fell for just a brief moment, and then the air caught beneath the wings and she soared through the treetops like a phantom. It took all her strength and concentration to keep the glider on a straight path to the compound roof, and when her feet touched the ground her muscles were fatigued and her skin coated with perspiration.

She hit another button on the long metal tube and the glider folded itself back up until it was small enough to fit back in her pack.

The body of the first sentry she'd shot lay face down in the greenish-blue water of the swimming pool. A hazy cloud of blood ballooned from under him, and his arms and legs floated like waving ribbons.

Her eyes and ears were alert, but all that greeted her was growing darkness and silence. Even the animals and birds in the jungle knew something bad was about to go down.

Grace unhooked the harness and pulled her SIG from a thigh holster. She stood silently next to the gray door that led from the roof down a set of stairs to the main floors of the house. Two heartbeats passed before she opened the door and slipped inside. It was quiet, but that wasn't unusual at this time of the day according to her intel—six sentries on duty surrounding the compound, only two guarding Vasquez's private suite of rooms.

Vasquez's stupidity only made her job easier.

Grace walked silently down the thickly carpeted hallway as if she weren't about to steal the schematics for a new superweapon—a weapon that used state-of-the-art laser technology—and sell it to another country. But the closer she got to Vasquez, the more her spine tingled in awareness that something was wrong. That tingle had saved her life more than once, and she never ignored it.

The hallway opened up into a landing just as she reached Vasquez's private rooms. Weak light filtered through the windows and cast rainbows as it pierced the glass chandelier that hung overhead.

She saw firsthand exactly why her spine was tingling.

Both sentries were slumped against each other—a dead man's embrace—one with a broken neck and the other with a hunting knife in his carotid. Efficient work considering the size of the sentries.

She pushed the bodies out of her way with her foot and eased the door open, her trigger finger at the ready on her SIG. All that mattered was the flash drive. If she didn't produce it, then she didn't get paid.

She crept into the room. The smells of new death were thick and cloying in the heat, and she could taste the fresh blood in the back of her throat with every breath she took. Dust motes danced in the air, and long shadows were cast in the fading sunlight.

Grace waited for her eyes to adjust and listened for sounds of footsteps, but all she heard was the gentle whir of the wicker fans that rotated slowly on the ceiling. She moved silently, staying close to the wall as she checked his suite.

Vasquez's bedroom was bigger than her whole apartment—the furniture oversized and ornate, the colors garishly red. He was set up for sex. The interesting kind of sex by the looks of things. Restraints and various whips and other tools lined one whole wall, and torn condom packages littered the floor. It looked like Vasquez had a busy day. Too bad his afternoon hadn't turned out so hot.

Gemino Vasquez's body lay spread-eagle on his bed. He was naked, and his eyes were open and unseeing. Two shots to the center of the forehead screamed of a professional hit. He hadn't been dead long. She couldn't stop the bitter disappointment when she saw the flash drive was gone from the chain on his right wrist.

"Hell," she whispered and moved to check the covers of his bed, just to make sure it hadn't come off in the struggle. But she knew in her heart it was long gone. Professionals didn't leave loose ends behind. And this was definitely professional. What ticked her off even more was that whoever did it managed to sneak in right under her nose. He had to have known she was watching through her scope and snuck in through the one blind spot she had at the back of the compound.

The stir of air behind her was the only warning she had before an arm locked around her throat.

"Looking for this?" a deep voice whispered in her ear. He held the flash drive in front of her face.

He pressed close against her back and squeezed his arm tighter around her throat so she had to breathe shallowly through her nose. Grace winced as he pressed his fingers against the pressure points of her wrist, and her pistol fell uselessly to the floor with a dull thunk.

Fear never had a chance to take hold. It was anger that drove Grace. Anger that had kept her alive the last couple of years. And she knew how to wield it. She threw her head back and aimed her heel at his knee simultaneously. He dodged her blows as if he'd been expecting them, but the distraction was enough for him to loosen his grip. She swept her leg and brought him to his knees, reaching down for the knife in her boot. The blade gleamed once in the fading sunlight just before it was knocked out of her hand and across the room.

He outweighed her by close to eighty pounds, and he had a good eight inches on her in height. They grappled and rolled, each one blocking the other's strikes with only seconds to spare. It was a well-choreographed dance.

A familiar dance.

The surprise of recognition took her off guard, and she looked up into laughing blue eyes framed by thick, dark lashes she'd always been jealous of. She had time to register that he'd let his hair grow —a shaggy mane of ink black that curled just over his ears and collar, and a face that was covered in a short, stubbled beard—just before her legs went out from under her. She hit the carpet with a thud. A hard body pressed her into the floor, and he held her wrists captive above her head.

"Hello, darling." His breath whispered against her skin. "You've been practicing. Who's your new sparring partner?"

"Gabe," she said. "What do you want?" She bucked beneath him, annoyed at the familiarity of his weight on her.

"I want you, of course." His lips glanced

across her cheek to the corner of her mouth, and she sucked in a breath that brought her body even closer to his. After everything he'd done, he was still the only man who could make her feel less than whole when their bodies weren't fused together. She hated him for it. She hated herself for it.

"Go to hell." She struggled against him, but he shifted his weight to hold her down.

"I've been there, thanks." He cupped his hand against her cheek—gently—softly. "You still feel good against me. Stop wiggling and we'll talk. Don't you want to at least hear my offer? Especially since I did your dirty work for you."

She stilled her body and relaxed, hoping he'd get distracted long enough for her to make a move, and she spoke through gritted teeth. "I don't want anything you have to offer. Just give me the flash drive."

"I figure we have exactly four minutes to get out of this place before the new guards show up for the shift change and Armageddon begins. All I'm asking is that you come back with me and hear me out. If you decide to turn me down, then I'll give you the flash drive with no hard feelings, and you can claim your bounty."

Grace stared at him and tried to decide if he was bluffing. "You know I don't trust you."

"Yes, I believe you've told me that before," he said, his gaze hard. "But what I'm offering will pay more than double any of the jobs you've recently taken. Hear me out."

"Fine." She knew her options were limited. "What are we waiting for?"

"Our rendezvous point is on the other side of the border," he said, rolling off of her. She ignored the hand he reached out to help her up. "We've got twenty minutes to get there or we miss our ride."

Grace had no choice but to follow him out of one hell and into another.

About the Author

Liliana Hart is a *New York Times*, *USA Today*, and Publisher's Weekly bestselling author of more than eighty titles. After starting her first novel her freshman year of college, she immediately became addicted to writing and knew she'd found what she was meant to do with her life. She has no idea why she majored in music.

Since publishing in June 2011, Liliana has sold more than ten-million books. All three of her series have made multiple appearances on the New York Times list.

Liliana can almost always be found at her computer writing, hauling five kids to various activities, or spending time with her husband. She calls Texas home.

If you enjoyed reading this book, I would appreciate it if you would help others enjoy this book too.

Recommend it. Please help other readers find this book by recommending it to friends, readers' groups and discussion boards.

Review it. Please tell other readers why you liked this book by reviewing.

Connect with me online:
www.lilianahart.com

Also by Liliana Hart

Laurel Valley

Tribulation Pass

Redemption Road

Midnight Clear

JJ Graves Mystery Series

Dirty Little Secrets

A Dirty Shame

Dirty Rotten Scoundrel

Down and Dirty

Dirty Deeds

Dirty Laundry

Dirty Money

A Dirty Job

Dirty Devil

Playing Dirty

Dirty Martini

Dirty Dozen

Dirty Minds

Dirty Weekend

Dirty Looks

Addison Holmes Mystery Series

Whiskey Rebellion

Whiskey Sour

Whiskey For Breakfast

Whiskey, You're The Devil

Whiskey on the Rocks

Whiskey Tango Foxtrot

Whiskey and Gunpowder

Whiskey Lullaby

The Scarlet Chronicles

Bouncing Betty

Hand Grenade Helen

Front Line Francis

The Harley and Davidson Mystery Series

The Farmer's Slaughter

A Tisket a Casket

I Saw Mommy Killing Santa Claus

Get Your Murder Running

Deceased and Desist

Malice in Wonderland

Tequila Mockingbird

Gone With the Sin

Grime and Punishment

Blazing Rattles

A Salt and Battery

Curl Up and Dye

First Comes Death Then Comes Marriage

Box Set 1

Box Set 2

Box Set 3

The Gravediggers

The Darkest Corner

Gone to Dust

Say No More

Printed in Great Britain
by Amazon